The Brothers' War

MARSHALL'S STORY

KINGFISHER
a Houghton Mifflin Company imprint
222 Berkeley Street
Boston, Massachusetts 02116
www.houghtonmifflinbooks.com

First published in 2005
2 4 6 8 10 9 7 5 3 1

LIBRARY OF CONGRESS CATALOGING-IN-PUBLICATION DATA
has been applied for.

ISBN 0-7534-5795-4
ISBN 978-07534-5795-5

Printed in India
1TR/0105/THOM/SGCH/90NS

MY SIDE OF THE STORY

The Brothers' War

MARSHALL'S STORY

PATRICIA HERMES

KINGFISHER
BOSTON

Have you read Melody's side of the story?
If you haven't, flip back and read it first; if you have,
you can now read Marshall's side of the story!

Chapter One

It was late afternoon when we started homeward, trotting our horses briskly down the lane from Melody's house. When we were out of sight of the house, Jeffrey reined in and turned to me.

"You ever seen Melody mad like that before?" he asked.

"Nope. That look on her face when Hugo said he wanted to go to war just about made me laugh out loud. She looked like Ma in one of her furies."

"You think that's how all girls are about war?" Jeffrey asked.

"Maybe," I said. "But Melody's as brave as a boy."

"Usually," Jeffrey said.

I nodded. She is, usually—brave and smart, too. But about this, she just doesn't understand. How can we let the Yankees take away our land, our slaves, our homes even? Besides, they turned and ran at Fort Sumter, so if war came, it wouldn't be much of one.

Jeffrey smiled. "Never seen a girl who could handle a horse better. She's almost as good as Ma. But I guess war talk makes even brave people scared."

"You scared?"

Jeffrey shook his head. "No. To tell the truth,

I don't think Melody's scared either. I think it's something else."

We looked at one another. We each knew what the other was thinking, though neither of us had yet said it.

"Don't worry, little brother," Jeffrey said, using his riding crop to whisk at some flies that circled our horses' heads. "She's our cousin, our *sister* practically. No matter what happens, we're family."

The words sounded brave, but about this, I knew he was as troubled as I was. "You really think war is coming?" I asked. "And you really think no one will get hurt?"

"Well, not *no one*," Jeffrey said. "But we just show the northerners we're serious, and they'll back down, just like they did in South Carolina. Know what else?" He grinned at me. "Uncle James didn't like it when I said it, but I do think it will be great fun to have uniforms and our own regiment."

I thought back to the lecture Uncle James had given us last night. "He didn't approve of us, that's for sure," I said. "I just wish I could go too."

"Too young, little brother!" Jeffrey said.

"Not that young!" I said. "Thirteen is almost grown-up!"

"*Almost* thirteen might be almost grown-up," Jeffrey said, "but you're not even thirteen yet."

"I will be in a month."

"Two months," Jeffrey said. "Then maybe you could be a bugle boy."

"Yeah," I said. "But you know Ma. She'd never let me."

"I'll put in a good word for you," Jeffrey said.

"You will?" I said.

"I will." Jeffrey grinned at me. "If you do my chores for a week."

I shook my head. "No, sir! Ma wouldn't let me go anyway, you know that. I should have been born first, then you'd see what it's like to be treated like a baby."

Jeffrey shrugged. "Ma worries. She's supposed to. That's what mothers do. Know what else?"

"What?"

"She'll take a riding crop to us if we don't get on home," Jeffrey said.

I tightened the reins and clicked my tongue at Moscow, and we started up again. The day was wonderfully clear, the sun making splashes of light through the leaves. Above us, birds and squirrels chittered, and every little while a chipmunk or a field mouse skittered across our path, making Moscow spook and rear up. Out on the flats Moscow is confident, tearing along like the wind. But he gets spooked easy in the woods.

We were quiet for awhile, riding along companionably, each of us buried in our own thoughts. I was wishing that I could go along with Jeffrey if he went. I don't mean that I want to shoot someone. But if it turns out to be just a little skirmish, it could be a real lark, and we'd be heroes. Ma might even treat me like a grown-up, instead of like the little brother.

After a minute Jeffrey turned to me. "You know how brothers like competitions?" he said.

"Like you and me?" I said because I knew what was coming—a dare, a wager.

"Bet my little brother can't shoot that crow up ahead," Jeffrey said, pointing to a huge pine tree where a crow sat at the very top, outlined against the sky.

"Oh, give me something harder," I said.

Jeffrey looked around. "All right, a moving target." He pointed with his crop to a squirrel darting from branch to branch above us.

"It's a bet," I said.

Both of us had our rifles crossways in front of us, and we reined in our horses. Slowly, I lifted my rifle to my shoulder, following the movement of the squirrel. When I had him in my sights, I took aim. There was a terrific bang. Moscow reared and did a backward dance as the squirrel fell to the ground in front of us.

And I hadn't even shot my rifle! I turned to Jeffrey.

"Quicker than you, little brother," he said laughing.

"Not fair!" I said. "You said *moving target*. You didn't say who could be *faster*."

Jeffrey laughed again. "Then here's another wager."

He looked around. The shot had scared off the rest of the wildlife, and for just those few moments, everything was still in the woods—no more chattering squirrels, no birds, just silence.

"Tether our horses," Jeffrey said. "We'll stand side by side by that old beech tree there. When something darts out—deer, fox, woodchuck, squirrel—we aim. That gives us both the same vantage point, the same chance."

"What's the wager?" I asked. I leaped down from Moscow and tethered him to a tree, and Jeffrey did the same. We picked up our rifles and walked to the beech.

"You do my chores for a week," he said. "Or I do yours."

"A whole week?"

"A whole week," Jeffrey said.

I hadn't accepted that wager before, but on this one, I stood an even chance. Jeffrey is a terrific shot—like he'd just proven. But I'm not too bad either.

"Wager accepted!" I said.

We stood under the tree. The woods that had been silent all around us slowly came back to life with little whisperings and chatterings and scurryings. We stood absolutely still, our rifles ready. Off to my left, I heard rustling and saw leaves moving in the underbrush. I raised my rifle. Jeffrey lifted his. Nothing.

We waited.

A partridge waddled out across the path directly in front of us. My gun was on my shoulder, I was squinting—and before I fired, the bird was down.

"Ooh," Jeffrey said, smiling as he went to retrieve the bird. "How nice to sleep late tomorrow."

I made a face at him as we went back to our horses. Jeffrey picked up the squirrel he had shot earlier, holding it up by its back paws. "Right through the eye," he said. He put it into his saddlebag along with the partridge. Pa taught us that if we kill a creature, we must use it, that it's a sin to kill for no reason. These two would probably end up in a stew.

We mounted our horses again, Jeffrey smiling and humming, me mad at myself. Why had I taken that bet? I'm a good shot, but I know Jeffrey is better. One good thing, though—if Jeffrey did go to war, he'd be able to hold his own on a battlefield. Jeffrey's so good at so many things. He's handsome, too, grown-up looking lately, and I noticed yesterday that Melody was looking at him differently too. I sighed. He'd ride off to war and glory, and I'd stay home doing his chores.

"Marshall?" Jeffrey said when we were almost home. "Let's not tell Pa what Uncle James said to us."

I looked over at him.

"You know," Jeffrey said. "About war and brother killing brother, that kind of thing."

I nodded. "I know," I said, and I voiced the thing we'd both been thinking but that neither had said aloud before. "Pa thinks Uncle James is on our side. Or if he has his doubts, he thinks he'll come around, and . . ."

"And," Jeffrey said, "I'd wager this horse underneath me that won't happen."

Well, I wasn't about to make any more bets with Jeffrey. But I was pretty darn sure that he was right.

Chapter Two

I had worked so hard for a week that I was blessed relieved when the following Monday came and my week of double chores was over. Ma thought it was the funniest thing ever when she heard about our wager, and she had no pity for me, not slacking off on my chores at all. I fell into bed exhausted each night. Chucking in the hay for the cattle was the hardest part. The hay was heavy, and with Jeffrey's cows added to mine, I now had 60 each morning and 60 again each night. On the last morning Ma came to the barn when I was just starting. She took the pitchfork from me, pushing me aside with her shoulder. "Go on now," she said. "I'll finish. But I hope this teaches you not to make wagers you can't win!"

"Thanks, Ma!" I said. I stood back, wiping my face on my sleeve, watching Ma as she tossed in the hay. I saw the way her shoulders moved, the muscles rippling under the skin. Ma is as strong as any man, maybe as brave, and certainly as outspoken. Sometimes I think she should have been born a man.

She turned then. "Stand there any longer," she said, "and I'm putting you back to work."

"I'm going, I'm going," I said.

I ran back to the house, got my rifle, and took off

for my friend Claude's house. I knew he'd want to go hunting. That's mostly the way Claude's family gets fed anymore, since their pa died some years back after falling off a horse.

Claude was doing his own chore when I got there, watching one of his many little brothers while playing with their old dog, Nanny. As soon as he saw me, gun in hand, he handed off the little one to his brother Cameron and got his own gun. Bringing home food was the most important chore, and Claude was the best at it.

Together, we walked along an old cattle trail and then came to a field and woods surrounded by low, wooden fencing. We stepped over the fence carefully, our rifles held crossways in front of us.

"Cameron says this here's old Indian territory," Claude said.

"You ever seen an Indian here?" I said.

Claude shook his head. "No. But Cameron prowls these woods like an Indian himself. He says he meets up with one once in awhile."

"I suspect Indians would make good spies," I said, thinking about what Pa had said about the need to recruit spies.

Claude nodded. We went quietly for awhile, keeping our eyes out for game. I listened to the sounds of the stream tumbling, the birds whistling from the treetops. I like being with Claude. He's quiet, and I always feel peaceful and quiet too when I'm with him. Sometimes we go an hour or more without talking but still feeling real friendly like. Today, though, this war business was working on my insides. I had started thinking about the way Jeffrey talked about war and the very different way Uncle James talked about it. It made me want to ask Claude. He's smart, even though he hasn't been to school since his pa died, doesn't even know how to read, but he thinks deep about things.

We stepped into the shade of trees that overarched a path made by animals walking to the water. It was very, very quiet there, so when I spoke, I felt like I should speak softly. "There going to be war, you think?" I asked.

Claude nodded.

"Will your brothers go?"

Claude shook his head. "No money."

"Oh," I said because I had forgotten. In order to sign up, you had to bring your own horse and buy your own uniform. With them being so poor, of course they couldn't go. They don't even own a horse, just an old mule for farming. Most folks nowadays wouldn't think it charity if someone gave them a horse, not if it was for the war. But who would give a horse to Claude's family? Truth was, most folks around didn't have much use for the Crawford family, thinking them shiftless. I knew differently, though. It wasn't their fault that their pa got killed. They did their best and took real good care of each other, took care of their ma, too. I rarely saw her, and Claude never spoke much about her, except to say that she was either feeling well or feeling poorly. Most days, she was feeling poorly.

"Cameron says he's going anyway," Claude said.

"Without a horse?" I asked.

Claude shrugged. "Knowing the woods like he does, maybe he'd do better on foot. He could be a scout."

Yes, he could. Cameron is a loner, a real woodsman, though there wasn't much chance that any outfit would take him without a horse.

We went on deeper into the woods, neither of us saying more, still looking out for game. Suddenly, a jackrabbit appeared, leaping across a small stream in front of us. Claude lifted his rifle and fired. The rabbit was still in midstride when it fell. Claude walked up, picked it up by its ears, and held it up to inspect it. It was dead for sure, and I was glad about that. Sometimes they were shot but still alive and quivering and looking at you with those scared old eyes. When they do that, I have to look away.

Claude slung the rabbit into the sack he had brought along, and we started up again, our eyes roving from side to side. One rabbit wouldn't make much of a meal for Claude's family, not with ten boys to feed—and every one of them with a first name that started with a "C." Seems to me that when it came to names, their mama had no imagination at all.

A moment later I saw a fat squirrel on a tree branch above us, its tail whisking back and forth. I squinted up into the tree, aimed, and shot. No squirrel fell to the earth, though. Instead it took off, leaping from branch to branch above our heads, chattering and scolding. I looked over at Claude, wondering if he'd be laughing, but he wasn't. We just shouldered our rifles and started off again.

"Could you kill a man?" I asked then because that was worrying me a lot.

Claude shook his head. "No."

"What if he was going to shoot you first?"

Claude turned to look at me. There was a rotted, bumpy log in front of us, and he lifted his foot to step over it. That's when I saw it—the snake, curled round and round, its head up, tongue flicking in and out.

"Stop!" I yelled. I flung my arm out and knocked

Claude backward—but not far enough or fast enough. His foot came down on the far side of the log, and the snake struck. Claude fell, sitting on the log, his leg still sticking out in front of him. The cobra reared to strike again.

I turned my gun around and struck at the snake with the butt of the gun. Hard. It squirmed and fell back, but its head was still weaving. It reared to strike once more. Again, I brought the butt of my gun down on it. I struck again and again and again until the snake lay still.

I turned to Claude. I was panting, and my heart was racing. "Did it get you?" I asked.

"Don't think so," he said. He tugged hard on his shoe, pulling it off, and then turned his foot over. The bottom of his foot was hardened and coarse, and in the center of the heel was a dark purplish spot. Claude touched his finger to the spot and then looked at the finger. No blood, and I was awful glad for that. He turned the shoe over. There was a hole in the bottom where the snake had struck, and he poked his finger around in the hole. "Didn't go clear through," he said. "Just a mean bruise."

He put the shoe back on, and when he was finished, the two of us stood and looked down at the snake. It was huge, as long as a yardstick and some more besides. Even flat-out dead like that, it was one scary-looking snake.

"Guess I do better with the butt end of the gun than with the shooting end," I said.

Claude smiled, but he didn't argue with me. "It's all right. You brought us supper," he said. He pulled out his knife then, and with one swift motion, he cut off the snake's head. He lifted the body and held it up. It was even bigger than I had thought and mighty heavy, too, from the way he was staggering under it. I helped him stuff it in his bag along with the rabbit.

"Snake stew," he said. "Clovis cooks it up with field onions. It'll feed us good tonight."

"Clovis cooks?" I asked.

"Best cook of the bunch."

"Better than your ma?" I asked.

Claude nodded.

I was feeling worn-out then, maybe from being scared about the snake, maybe from being exhausted from a week of double chores. "Head back now?" I asked Claude.

He nodded.

We walked along, with Claude limping a bit, but he wouldn't let me carry the sack, even though I offered. After awhile Claude said, "If there's war, it's not going to be about slavery, you know."

"I know," I said. "It's about lots of things—slavery, states' rights, new territories. Pa says it's especially about the north not bullying us around."

Claude shook his head. "None of those things," he said. "It's about money. And only a fool dies for money."

Suddenly, I felt anger rising inside me. I didn't care what he said about his brother, but my brother wasn't a fool. And neither were Melody or Uncle James, although they were fools for being on the other side—if they were.

"My brother's not a fool," I said hotly.

Claude shifted the sack to his other hand and rested his arm on my shoulder for a moment. I've never known Claude to say an angry word, and now wasn't any different.

"I know your brother's not a fool," he said quietly. "Neither is mine. I just don't see the sense in this. It's foolish to war about whose side is right and whose is wrong."

"But you got to fight for what's right," I said.

Claude turned to look at me. "You ever hear what Mr. Lincoln said about that?"

"No."

"Mr. Lincoln said, 'I don't know if God is on my

side. I just pray that I'm on his side.'"

"Well," I said, "Mr. Lincoln is sure on the wrong side."

"Still," Claude said, "it kinda makes you think, don't it?"

Chapter Three

It did make me think. But it didn't stop me from wishing I could go with Jeffrey. He had joined up with the 17th Regiment along with six friends. He'd gotten himself outfitted with a sleeping roll, cooking utensils, gun and sword, and everything. And of course, he had a horse. That's because Pa had money and so did the other boys' fathers, money for arms and equipment and even for servants to go along with them. But a troop or regiment has to be a certain size to be full strength, and that was a problem. There weren't enough wealthy men around, so there weren't enough troop members available.

That didn't stop Jeffrey and them from getting ready, though, and even practicing troop movements. Two nights a week, Tuesday and Thursday, they went on exercises, romping with their horses on a field in the center of town. Some nights I went along, just sat on the side watching. Other nights, I sat astride Moscow, fidgeting at the edge of the field, praying that just once Jeffrey would call me in to take the place of one of the boys, practicing shooting or fence jumping or something. He never did, though.

One Tuesday night when we got there Claude and his two oldest brothers, Cash and Clovis, were sitting on a bench, watching. There were other boys there too from around the county, boys Jeffrey's age watching, looking envious. They cheered on the boys, and some of them yelled the Rebel yell. Once I yelled along with them so loud that it made Moscow rear back. I dismounted then and tethered Moscow and went to sit with Claude. Clovis and Cash both nodded at me, though neither of them spoke.

"Who's the troop leader?" Claude asked.

"They haven't chosen yet," I said. "I hope it's Jeffrey. Then maybe I could sign on as bugle boy."

"You'd really go?" Claude asked.

"If Ma let me. I don't know if she would, though." I tilted my head toward Cash and Clovis. "They want to go?"

Claude nodded. "Yeah, Cameron, too. All of them."

Both Clovis and Cash were leaning forward on the bench, their elbows on their knees, speaking quietly to one another, their mouths barely moving. I wondered if they were talking about joining up. It made me sad thinking that they wanted to but didn't have the money and probably wouldn't take money, being so proud and all. Yet lots of folks were helping other people join up. Like Ma—she was getting donations of horses and cattle for the troops. Ever since the start of summer, she's worked at that, even though most folks think that isn't at all proper for a woman to do. Ma, though, she doesn't give a hoot what people think. She's been badgering and bullying each family into giving something four-footed. She's even been after our minister, but so far, he's been standing fast against her, says he has but the one horse. Everybody in the county suspects that maybe he's really a Union sympathizer.

Well, if folks were giving cattle and horses and nobody thought that was charity, then why couldn't they take uniforms and guns? I remembered how Pa had outfitted Jeffrey, and suddenly, I had an idea. I wondered if I could talk Pa into outfitting the whole troop. That way it wouldn't seem like charity, not if all the boys were being outfitted.

As soon as the boys had finished their maneuvers—and I have to say, they didn't look like they were very organized to me—I said good night to Claude and started on home. Jeffrey didn't come with me because he stayed with his regiment friends, and they went to the saloon like they do each night after practice.

As soon as I got home, I went to the library. Pa was reading something aloud to Ma, and he stopped when I came in.

"Marshall," he said. "This is momentous. I was reading this to your ma, and I want you to hear it too.

It's the resignation letter that General Lee sent to Mr. Lincoln. He sent it on to me, too. Everything's going to change now."

Pa turned up the lamp, smoothed the piece of paper, and adjusted his reading glasses. "This is what he writes to Mr. Lincoln: 'Sympathizing with you in the troubles that are pressing so heavily upon our beloved country and entirely agreeing with you in your notions of allegiance etc., I have been unable to make up my mind to raise my hand against my native state, my relations, my children, and my home. I have therefore resigned my commission in the army and never desire again to draw my sword save in defense of my state.'"

Pa removed his glasses and looked at us. "And do you know something?" Pa went on. "In the attached letter General Lee tells me that just two days ago—two days!—Mr. Lincoln offered him the command of the *federal* armies."

In the dim light I could see Ma smiling. "If Mr. Lincoln wanted him, then we can assume that General Lee's a brilliant leader."

Pa raised his eyebrows.

"Yes," Ma said. "Give the devil his due. Mr. Lincoln has a good head on his shoulders." She leaned forward. "You'll do the same, Mr. Gordon?" she said quietly, using that formal way of speaking that she only does when she's most serious. "You'll resign?"

Pa nodded, but he looked troubled. He rubbed his eyes, ran a hand down his face and over his neatly trimmed little beard, shaking his head. "When I graduated from West Point, I couldn't imagine such a day ever coming to me. And I can assure you that General Lee is also heartily against secession."

"Then why is he doing what he's doing?" I asked.

Pa and Ma both turned to me, surprised looking, as though they had forgotten I was there. "Son," Pa said, "Virginia is our home, our heart. You heard General Lee's words." Pa picked up the letter again. "'Unable to raise my hand against my native state, my relations, my children, my home.'" Pa laid down the letter. "How could I turn and fight against our neighbors, our families, our own land?"

I thought of saying *but Uncle James is family*, but I didn't. It surely was confusing, though.

We were quiet awhile, and then Pa said, "What worries me is that we're going to be outnumbered. The Union armies will have thousands more men than we do. We're going to need every able-bodied man we can find."

Well, they couldn't have given me a better chance to speak. "I know how you can raise troops," I said.

"There were a dozen boys in town tonight, wishing like anything that they had horses and money. They didn't know I was listening, but I heard one boy say he'd shoot his own mother if he thought he'd get money that way."

"He'd *what*?" Ma said.

"It was just a boast, a joke," I said. "But they'd all go if they had money and horses."

"I'm aware of that," Ma said. "I've got promises of over twenty horses so far."

"But they need equipment," I said. "Couldn't you outfit Jeffrey's entire troop? I mean, suppose that not just Jeffrey and the rich boys but *all* the boys got *all* the equipment from some committee—like you maybe? Then no one would have to feel like it was charity. You know how folks hate charity."

"What folks are you talking about?" Pa asked.

I was afraid of this. It's so unfair that everyone thinks the Crawfords are lazy and shiftless, and I was pretty sure that Ma and Pa thought so too. I just shrugged. "All those boys," I said. "All the ones milling around the town square tonight that I just told you about. Every one of them wants to go."

Ma turned to Pa. "Actually, Marshall's got a good idea. It would increase the size of our local militia, at the very least. There's no sense not looking out for our own."

Pa turned to me, tugging at his beard awhile. "I'll consider it," he said. "Yes, I'll do that. And maybe I'll find a way for you to help too."

"Me?" I said. "You mean I can go?"

"Absolutely not!" Ma objected.

Pa shook his head. "Not go fight. But from what you've been telling me about 'overhearing' tonight, I think you'd make one devil of a good spy."

I looked down at my hands in my lap, trying not to smile. I wouldn't be left behind! Jeffrey wouldn't be the only one to help. I'd be *one devil of a good spy.*

Chapter Four

It took only around two weeks before Jeffrey's regiment was up to strength and ready to move on to Alexandria. There, Pa said, they'd be deployed to defend the city. Looking at all the boys' gear, I was so proud of Pa. He had outfitted every single one, including two of Cameron's brothers, Clovis and Cash. The troop leader—and it didn't turn out to be Jeffrey but was his best friend, Marcus—said that two boys of the same family were enough because there were many other families whose sons wanted to go. That meant that Cameron, who was too young, had to stay behind.

He was just about heartbroken. I was, too, not just for him but for myself. I begged to be allowed to go as a bugle boy, but Ma wouldn't hear a word about it. Even Jeffrey pleaded with her for me, but all she'd say was, "Too young, too young, too young!"

It made me mad, but I comforted myself with what Pa had said—that I'd be put to use as a spy. Besides, there was no sense arguing once Ma had made up her mind. Actually, I think Ma would have gone herself if she could. A battle was looming, and from all of the rumors, it would take place near Bull Run, practically outside our back door.

For weeks after Jeffrey left we heard the sounds of guns and troop movements as the Union army massed along the Potomac river. Pa had met several times with General Lee but hadn't left to join yet, and I figured there must be a reason. Then one day everything grew quiet, an awesome quiet, a sure sign, Pa said, that Union troops were ready, just waiting to cross the Potomac and take Alexandria under cover of night. Many of the Virginia militias, even Jeffrey's regiment, had begun abandoning Alexandria, pulling back toward us. On that quiet morning Pa said he needed to see Alexandria for himself—and he invited me along!

We were at the breakfast table when Pa announced it, and Ma set down her coffee cup with a clatter. "Marshall?" she said. "That little mouse?" She shot a little smile at me when she said it, though.

"Ma!" I said.

"General Lee needs information, and a man won't do," Pa said. "Marshall has a good eye for detail and an ear for listening. Besides, he's small and a child can slip through unnoticed."

Well, at least there was something good about being Jeffrey's *little* brother. My heart started thudding heavily inside me, though. Slip through where? Could I really help, and what was I supposed to be spying on?

"I want him to go to Jim Jackson," Pa went on. "Jim can tell him what's happening in town."

Oh, yes! I've been to the Marshall House many times with Pa to meet with his friend, Jim Jackson. I've watched the two of them spreading out maps, talking about slavery and the new territories, and, lately, talking about what they thought of President Lincoln—which wasn't much.

"Well," Ma said, "a tavern's one sure place to get all the news. It'll be dangerous?"

Pa shook his head. "Not really." He turned and winked at me. "Unless it's dangerous for the boy to have his first whiskey."

I smiled, and for the first time in my life, I felt like Pa was seeing me as a man—or almost a man. Ma turned to me then. I sat up tall, trying to look grown-up and brave, as brave as Jeffrey, but it was hard to hold back a grin. After a long moment of frowning at me Ma nodded. "All right. But if you're big enough to do a man's job, then you're big enough to take care of your pa, you hear me? Anything happens to him, I'll box your ears."

"I'll watch out for him, Ma," I said, smiling.

"And don't you dare have a whiskey!" Ma said, and there was no laughter in her voice when she said that.

"Yes, ma'am," I said.

It was late in the day when Pa and I started out. We had our rifles and food and water in our saddlebags. It was a long ride, almost two hours, and it was just about dark when we got close to Alexandria. There we stopped on the hill overlooking the Potomac. Spread out below us was the Union army, and Pa was right—they were on the move. Swarms of them had crossed to our side, and more were coming—in boats, on horseback, across the bridges. Horses, artillery, men, cannons, all swept toward us in a long procession, as far as the eye could see. But what was so very strange about it was how orderly it seemed, orderly and silent. There was no firing, just the sound of marching feet and horses whinnying and the rustle and hubbub of movement. Occasionally there was a whispered command, and then all was still again.

"It's so quiet, Pa," I said. "What's happening?"

"We're letting them take Alexandria," Pa said softly. "Our militia is no match for them. We can't defend, and we don't want them to destroy the city. Remember this, though, it's a first skirmish. The Union has thrown in so many troops because they're defending the capital. That means they're spread thin elsewhere. Our time will come."

"But they're taking over!"

"For now," Pa said. "Just for now. General Lee planned this."

I looked at Pa, wondering how he knew all of this, but I knew he had his ways. We were quiet for awhile, just watching. It had gotten truly dark, but with all the fires and light from the torches, we could see much of what was going on. It was just awesome, all those men and equipment, all moving so silently.

"There's Marshall House," Pa said, pointing to the tavern below us.

I nodded. I could see the flag of the Confederacy flying over it, bright in the light of some torches.

"When you go down there," Pa said, "go in and find Jim Jackson—nobody else, just Jim. Tell him I need all the latest news—how many troops, how many guns, how many ships, anything he can tell you quickly without causing suspicion. If he can write it down, all the better. If not, keep it in your head. Keep your eyes and ears open too. You know how to eavesdrop."

"Yes, sir!" I said, my heart already thumping hard thinking about making my way through those troops.

Like Pa was reading my mind, he said, "You're just a little boy. You were sent by your ma to find your pa in the tavern."

I squinted up my eyes. "*Sir*?" I said.

"Your ma is real worried about your pa," Pa said. "He's been gone so long, and your pa, well, he's a good man, but your ma says he has a habit of drinking. You've been sent to bring him home."

"Oh," I said, and I felt rather dumb that it had taken me so long to figure out what Pa meant. I laughed. "All right," I said. "I can do it."

Pa pulled out his pocket watch. "An hour," he said. "If you're not back in an hour, I'm going down for you. Be careful, son."

"I'll be careful," I said, and I made my way through the scrub and scurried down the hillside and into the town. I've been there many times before, but it was odd, walking there now, everything so different. I passed the Episcopal school where Ma had gone, but it was shuttered, as if all the pupils had been sent away long ago. Even the churches were silent and shuttered. Yet all around were soldiers setting up camp right in the square and townspeople walking around, almost like they were sightseeing. It seemed like half the town was barricaded behind closed doors, and the other half had come out to see what was happening. I saw some families who were moving away, pushing wheelbarrows piled high with household goods as they went toward the train depot. There was even a sutler, one of those men who follow the troops with a wagon, selling pies and newspapers and other things soldiers might want. Nobody took notice of me among all the folks milling around.

I went directly to the tavern and pushed open the door. Inside was a swarm of men, Union soldiers and townspeople both. Just as I came in, a Union officer strode toward the stairs that led to the floors above. Another man was with him, a Union guard, it seemed like. Union soldiers in uniform were cheering them on, shouting, "Cheers for Colonel Ellsworth! Cheers for Ellsworth!" Hurrying along behind them was my pa's friend Mr. Jackson. He looked very, very angry.

"Mr. Jackson, sir!" I called out.

Mr. Jackson didn't even look at me, just pushed past me and started up the stairs behind the Union officer.

"Mr. Jackson, sir?" I said again, and I hurried after him.

He paid me no mind. He climbed the stairs after the Union soldier, shouting up to him. "You stop there, sir! I say, halt!"

It was then that I saw that Mr. Jackson held a gun in his hand.

I started to back away, down the steps, away from them. And then, like what happens in a dream sometimes, things seemed to be spinning, slowly,

slowly. The Union officer, Colonel Ellsworth, reached the top of the steps. The Confederate flag flew just above him. He reached for it and tore it down. He turned with it in his hand, a smile breaking across his broad face.

Mr. Jackson raised his pistol. And fired.

The colonel's face disappeared in a bloom of blood. His body jerked, and blood spurted everywhere, across his coat, down his chest, and he tottered backward first and then forward, slowly, tumbling sideways.

I turned to look at Mr. Jackson. He looked stunned for a moment, his face turning from a deep red to ashen. He seemed to see me then, to recognize me. He pushed me backward toward the stairs, as if in suddenly recognizing me he also recognized that I was in danger. Before I could move toward the stairs, the Union guard raised his gun. There was a terrific noise, a blast in the closed stairway, and I put my hands over my ears. Mr. Jackson fell. Blood spurted from his mouth, his nose, and as he fell, I saw the kind of surprised look that crossed his face. Then both he and the officer tumbled down a few steps and lay at my feet. Dead.

Chapter Five

I don't know how I made it back to Pa. I moved without thought, just planting my feet one in front of the other. Nobody stopped me in the tavern, even though I was covered in blood. I had bent and tried to lift Mr. Jackson's head, but his eyes were blank, and I laid him down gently. My hands were bloody, and where I had held him against me, my shirt was thick with blood, sticky and sweet smelling.

I pushed my way outside along with other people, all of them shouting, some crying, some cheering. I heard a man yell something about the Yankees and a flag, and a huge melee sprang up in the courtyard of the tavern. All that earlier quiet had become an uproar.

I was elbowing my way through the crowd when suddenly I was grabbed by the back of my shirt, and someone spun me around. A big man in a Union uniform, his face red, his beard and mustache reddish too, was peering closely into my face. He thrust me away then, disgusted looking. "Just a kid!" he shouted over his shoulder.

I turned away, my heart thumping hard, but had gone only a few steps when I was grabbed again. "Wait! What's this?" he said, spinning me around again to face him. It was the same Union soldier, and he was looking down at my shirt and hands—and at his hands, now covered with blood.

"It's nothing!" I said. "I . . . I just had an accident."

"Accident!" he said. He turned and called over his shoulder. "Thomas! Over here. Is this the one?" He was holding my shirtfront tight, but as he turned to speak his grip loosened a bit, and I twisted away from him, pulling my shirt from his hands.

"Hey!" he yelled. "Get back here!"

I didn't. I took off running hard, running, my breath catching in my throat. I didn't think I could run another step, but I kept going, and maybe it was God himself who was thrusting me ahead, I don't know. All I know is that within a few minutes I was away from town, running silently and alone, no one thundering after me.

As I scrambled to the top of the hillside, I kept looking behind and then stopping to wipe my hands on the grass, but I couldn't get rid of the feel or the smell of the blood. "Help me, Lord," I whispered. "Help me." Once I slipped, my feet going right out from under me in the dewy grass. I lay there for a moment catching my breath, my eyes closed, but the images of those two bloody men were there along the insides of my eyelids, and I quickly opened my eyes again. A sliver of moon hung in the sky, and I looked behind me. No one chasing me. Maybe they had decided that I wasn't important after all. And then I remembered—I hadn't gotten any information, none at all! I had failed in my first important job. Should I have stopped and asked someone else? Surely I knew enough townspeople; maybe I should have looked for them. Should I turn and go back? But no, it was too late.

I remembered Pa and tried to calm myself. It was his friend who was dead. I had to be calm for him. I came to the top of the incline. The horses must have heard me because they began snuffling and whinnying softly, and I saw Pa stand and move toward the edge of the incline.

"Son?" he called out softly.

"Pa?" I cried. "Pa."

"What is it," he said. "What happened?" He took me by my shoulders. I was trembling so hard my teeth were chattering. "Here," Pa said, and he eased me to the ground as waves of nausea flooded over me. Pa hurried to his saddlebags and came back with a flask. He poured some of the liquid into the cap and held it out to me. "Here's that whiskey I promised you," he said. "Easy now."

I couldn't take it. Nausea swept over me, and I

turned my head, crawled a little way away, and I vomited. When I was finished, I crept back to Pa, exhausted. Pa poured water from his canteen and cleaned my face and hands. He kept murmuring to me, "You're here, it's all right."

I sat trembling and shivering, and Pa wrapped his jacket around me. Finally, I was able to talk, to tell him what had happened. He didn't interrupt, didn't ask questions, just listened until I had said everything there was to say. When I was finished, he handed me the whiskey.

"Ma said I shouldn't," I whispered.

"It's medicine," Pa said. "You need it. Slowly now."

I took a sip and almost choked, the liquid burning my throat. After a moment or two, though, I did feel better, the blood returning to my head.

"They are both dead?" Pa asked then. "You're sure about that?"

I almost wanted to laugh. If he had seen what I had seen . . . But all I said was, "Yes, sir."

"You ready enough to ride now?" Pa asked.

"Pa, I didn't get the information you wanted! Should I have asked someone else?"

"You did get information, son," Pa said. "We know what happened, and we're the first to know. I'll get a message to General Lee, and he'll take action. Things are going to get a whole lot worse, and it's going to happen quickly. This won't go down easily on either side. Let's go on to your Uncle James."

"Uncle James?" I said. "It's the middle of the night!"

"Yes," Pa said. "But a Union colonel's been shot to death. Jim Jackson, one of the best-known men around—best-loved, too—is shot dead, though why in the world Jim did what he did, I'll never know. Now we're truly at war." Pa leaned down, giving me a hand up. "Let's ride."

We rode side by side, our horses making little clippety-clop sounds, sometimes striking a pebble or rock and making a sharper sound. I made myself focus on the sounds, as well as other sounds of the night, owls calling to one another, crickets, and frogs. I remembered how when Melody was little, she said that foggy nights were froggy nights, and ever since, we always call them that. I wished the sun would come up and the birds would sing, would push back the dark and the pictures from the tavern that ran around inside my head.

As we neared Melody's, I knew I had to tell Pa something, and I rode up alongside him. "Pa," I said. "You know how Jeffrey and I were at Melody's a few weeks ago?"

"Yes," Pa said. "You two came back so tight-lipped that I knew something happened. I figured you'd tell me when you were good and ready."

"Well, see, from the way Uncle James and Melody talked, I don't think they're on our side."

"I know that, son," Pa said. "Believe me, I know my brother. But when he hears what happened tonight, he'll think again. He can't fight against his own state and home, not with that huge plantation of his. Now let's get on there."

We rode harder then, and soon we were trotting up the familiar drive to the house. A light was burning in the library, and we tethered our horses. By the time we had come around front to the porch, Uncle James had opened the door wide.

In the library I sank down on the couch, too overwhelmed to speak—to even listen, hardly. After awhile Melody came into the library, and I couldn't speak to her either. I just sat staring at my hands, at the blood that was caked around my fingernails. Pa told what had happened, and hearing it was like being back there again. After some time the talking seemed to be finished, and it was no surprise to me that Uncle James hadn't come around to Pa's side. Still, it made my heart ache something bad. Pa stood to leave, and I saw him wrap Melody in his arms and kiss her forehead.

I stood, too, and Uncle James came to me. He put both hands on my shoulders. "Be brave," he said quietly. "Be true to yourself. You're a good young man."

A *man?* Did men feel scared like I did?

"Go with God," Uncle James said, and he turned me to face Pa, who was already striding away down the hall.

I heard Melody calling to me then. "Marshall!" she said. "Marshall!"

I stopped. I wanted to turn back. I did. But the scene from the tavern was pasted on the back of my eyelids, running like a lantern slide show inside my head, those men being shot, dying, bleeding to death. Why? Because of what they believed in?

Melody and her papa. Me and my pa. What was anybody supposed to believe?

Chapter Six

It was nearing dinnertime a few days later when Pa sat going through papers at his library desk. Two of his friends from West Point, Colonel Washburn and his aide, were joining us for dinner, and I knew that Pa would huddle with them here in the library afterward. For now, though, both Ma and I were working here, Ma sewing, me studying the history of Virginia. Pa had insisted that I study for two hours each day, impressing on me the importance of being knowledgeable about the reasons for the war.

I turned pages, trying to pay attention, but nothing seemed to stick in my head. I kept remembering the scene at the tavern that night, the shouts, the smell of firearms and blood, the man who grabbed my shirt. I was tired all the time because I hardly slept, afraid that if I closed my eyes, the images would begin again. It wasn't just how awful that night was. It was that if this was war, it seemed to me we were just beginning. I really wanted to help, I did. Pa said I'd be one devil of a good spy. But could I ever do that again, see that again?

All of us sat quietly, the clock on the mantelpiece ticking the minutes away. Soon we heard the sound of horse hooves and voices chattering—the Negroes coming in from the fields for the noonday meal.

Ma stood then. "I'll go and see to Margaret, see that everyone's dinner is set out." She turned to me then. "You go to the pump and wash up. You look like something the cat dragged in."

I stood and closed my book and then went down the hall and out to the back pump to wash up. That's when I saw him—Hugo. He was on his horse, riding behind the wagon with the other Negroes, hanging back a little.

"Hugo!" I called to him. "What are you doing here?"

Hugo jumped off his horse, tethered him, and came to the pump. He looked around briefly and then grinned at me. "I was jes' riding the woods path and seen your darkies coming in for their noon meal. Decided to follow them and see how you all is doing."

"You're far from home!" I said. "How's Melody?"

"Oh, she misses you something bad. She pretends not to, but she does. She'd have my head if'n she knew I was telling you that, though. She acts real mad at you and Mr. Jeffrey."

"She probably is."

Hugo laughed. "She's madder'n a wet hen most days. You know her, keeps bothering me and bothering me, wants to help with the war, like there's anything a gal could do."

I laughed. "Knowing Melody, there's plenty that girl could do," I said. We stared at each other for a minute, and then we both looked away, both of us most likely thinking the same thing—that we were on opposite sides.

"How's Mr. Jeffrey?" Hugo asked.

"He's joined up," I said.

"That's all right then," Hugo said. "I got to go now. Sooner or later, I can tell her I saw you, and she'll be mighty glad."

"Why are you here?" I asked. "You're far from home."

"Passing by, that's all." He turned and started back to his horse.

"Hugo!" I called after him. "Wait! Stay awhile! Won't you eat? There's plenty here."

Hugo just shook his head and mounted his horse. "I'm mighty fine!" he said, waving.

I watched him ride off and then finished washing up. I was so glad to have seen him, so glad to hear about Melody, even if she was as mad as a wet hen—and I'd have been surprised if she wasn't. I went back inside the house, and we all sat down for dinner, Pa introducing us to Colonel Washburn and his aide. All through dinner the men talked earnestly about the war, and I listened and tried to learn, but the truth was, I was mostly bored. The war hadn't even really started, and already I was tired of it. We were just about finished eating and were pushing back from the table when Colonel Washburn turned to me. "Who was that little darkie I saw you talking with earlier?" he asked.

"Hugo?" I said. "That's just Hugo, my . . ." How could I explain what Hugo was to me? A Negro groom? A *friend*?

"Hugo came here?" Pa said, frowning. "What did he want?"

"Nothing!" I said. "Just to see how we are."

"Some of these darkies are spies," Colonel Washburn said. "Think they can ride through the woods, looking innocent. We've caught several taking messages and spying on troop movements." He turned to his aide. "Check up on that one. Find out who he is and what he's doing around here."

"You think Hugo's a *spy*?" I said.

I saw Pa frown at me, so I said, "Sorry, sir." But inside myself, I thought that was the silliest thing I had ever heard. Hugo's so chatty he couldn't keep a secret if his life depended on it. Still, I hated the idea of the General's men finding him and scaring him half to death with questions, though I realized there was nothing I could do about it now.

Pa went to the library with the men, and Ma and I went out to the porch. Ma was mending something, a dress for one of the maids it looked like, and I sat on the steps, staring off into the fields. I was thinking about that night at the tavern, seeing it play again in my head.

"What are you seeing out there?" Ma asked, and it was soft the way she said it, not her usual gruff way at all.

I just shrugged.

"Seeing that night all over again?" Ma asked.

I nodded. "Yeah," I said. "I can't forget it."

"Don't try," Ma answered.

"Why?" I said. "Everybody says you shouldn't think of bad things."

"Hogwash!" Ma said. "You stuff it down, it pops up somewhere else. Better to let it be and let it have a little air. Heals faster that way."

"You sure?" I said.

"Sure as I can be," Ma said.

I was quiet for a long while, and Ma was too. After awhile I said, "Do you know how much blood is inside you?"

Ma didn't answer for a minute. And then she said, "A lot, I imagine."

I nodded. "A lot."

Ma came and sat beside me on the steps. I had my hands folded between my knees, and Ma took my folded hands in hers. "You're a brave young man," she said.

"Not really," I said. "I was scared half to death."

"Only a fool is unafraid," Ma said. "Seems you're growing up right before my eyes."

"I am?" I said, surprised.

"You are," Ma said, and she went on holding my hands. And then I did something I haven't done in about a hundred years—I leaned my head against her, just like I used to do when I was a little kid. And do you know, even if I was growing up, still, it felt awful good to do.

Chapter Seven

By the middle of July it was clear that a huge battle was looming. Pa had been right that night when Colonel Ellsworth and Mr. Jackson were killed, when he said things would be different. They were. Everything turned, people turned against each other, armies geared up, skirmishes broke out everywhere. The Confederate army massed along the river at Bull Run, and the Union army massed nearby, just waiting to fight. Pa resigned his commission in the U.S. army and accepted a commission in the army of northern Virginia. He had already left to serve under General Beauregard, taking Matthew, his groom, with him. Before he left, though, he called me into the library.

"I'm going to be sending along messages to you," he said, his face grave. "There will be things I'll want you to find out for me. You can send answers through Matthew."

"Yes, sir," I said. "What kinds of things?"

"I don't know yet. But I'll need your eyes and ears."

"Yes, sir," I said again. A few weeks ago I had thought that being a spy was a lark. Not now, though. Death seemed to happen so easily!

Pa handed me a gun then, a small derringer. "Keep

it with you always," he said. "Times are dangerous. You're the man of the house now. But you don't need to let your ma know you have it, understand?" I nodded and took the gun, feeling proud that Pa trusted me with it but sad, too. Because, then, Pa was gone.

It was maybe the hottest summer ever, the sun beating down on our fields and on the house. The slaves got irritable and itchy, and that made Ma irritable and itchy. Some of our slaves had run off, and Ma was shorthanded in the house, and there weren't enough field hands, and that made everyone even more irritable. A few times Ma got so angry that she said she'd go out looking for them and beat their bottoms if she found them. Of course, she was only talking big. I've never seen her raise a hand to anyone, slave or anyone else. The only time she came close to beating anyone was the time when Jeffrey and me got into the grain bin and almost suffocated. After we were dug out Ma hugged us and hugged us and then started to take a paddle to our bottoms but instead ended up hugging us again.

Other days came, though, when Ma was calmer. "Let them go!" she said. "They'll see soon enough there's no such thing as free food and shelter anywhere in the world. Who's going to feed them as good as we feed them? They'll be back." And sure enough, two of the kitchen maids who had run away came dragging back to our door no more than two weeks after they'd left. Ma told them to go to their houses and get bathed, and she even found new dresses for them because the ones they were wearing were so dirty and torn up, you could almost believe they had been in a fight with raccoons. After that they crept around the kitchen working extra silently, trying extra hard to be helpful.

That was a good thing because Ma had all kinds of work for them and for everybody else, too. She was collecting horses and cattle for the troops. One day she even went out to the minister's field and counted his livestock—40 cows and scores of chickens and hens and four or five horses, though he said he had but the one horse. Sometimes I went along with Ma to badger folks. Sometimes they gave a cow or a horse right there on the spot, and I helped take it home in the wagon. Other times, folks promised to send it along. Sometimes they did, and sometimes they didn't. If they didn't, Ma just went after them the following week.

One day Ma and I took the carriage and went out to the hill where there was talk that a battle was looming. "Might as well see what everybody else is seeing," Ma said as we set out that morning with our picnic basket. "I'm planning on meeting some men who may be able to help us."

"Help with what?"

"Horses and cattle, what else?" Ma said. "The most important things a man or a woman can have. The army surely needs them."

We rode on quietly for awhile till we came to the hill where there were many carriages gathered. Below us, we could see the armies gathered, see the many wagons there. Something had been running around inside my head, something about Claude's brother Cameron. He was so determined to go to war, so disappointed that his brothers got to go and he didn't. "Ma," I said as we reined in our horses atop the hillside. "I know how to get a horse from Reverend Hunting."

"You do?" Ma said.

"If we get him to give us one, can I give it to Cameron so he can go too?"

"Don't see why not," Ma said.

"It means telling a bit of a lie," I said.

Ma laughed loudly. "Think that would worry me?"

I told her my plan, and she just roared with laughter. "Now where did you come up with that?" she asked. "I believe it might work. I can't wait for Sunday."

Ma and I were still laughing,when I looked down, and there, beside the carriage, looking as bright and beautiful and spunky as ever, was Melody.

"Melody!" I said. I jumped down, but before I could even speak, Ma had leaped from the wagon too and grabbed Melody up into her arms.

"Oh, my dear girl, I've missed you!" Ma said, hugging her tightly.

Ma held Melody away, looked in her face, and then pulled her close. They whispered together a moment, and I stood there just watching. I know that Ma is just one of the favorite people in Melody's world, and I could see their happiness now, both of them, see it written on their faces. For minutes—three, four—they went on talking so softly that I couldn't hear. Finally, when I couldn't stand being left out any longer, I stepped forward. "Can I join this party?" I said.

Ma laughed. She pushed Melody in my direction. "Go, talk!" she said, laughing. "Talk, talk, talk! You won't agree on anything, but go ahead and talk."

Well, Melody is a lot like Ma in some ways, outspoken and not a bit afraid of it. As soon as she turned away from Ma, she frowned at me. "Even your mother says war is dumb!" she said.

"She also says it's something we have to do."

"No!" Melody said. "She said it's something men are going to do anyway. Oh, I'm so angry at you! I believe you're the most misguided, misinformed boy I have ever met."

I looked up at Ma, thinking Ma would scold Melody for what she was saying, but Ma was busy talking with some men who had ridden up and wasn't paying any more attention to us.

Melody said more then, reminding me how I once said war would be a lark! Just like her. Can't let go of a thing. And then she turned away and went back to her own carriage. For a moment I thought of following her, of arguing some, but I stopped. She didn't approve of me, and I didn't approve of her, and Ma was right—we were going to war whether we wanted to or not.

For the rest of that week, though, it weighed heavier on my mind than usual. It's one thing to say you know what is right to fight for—and what is wrong. It's not so simple when it's your very own cousin and uncle fighting against your father and brother. By the following Sunday it was still aching inside my head, but I was also giddy with the thought of what Ma and I had planned for Reverend Hunting. We were in church, Ma and I, the two of us listening to the service. We stood to pray and sat to be preached at and stood to sing again. Reverend Hunting closed the service asking us all to stand and sing the hymn *Glory, Hallelujah*. We did, and it was lusty, bold singing, folks heartened by a song of such grace and glory.

As the service ended, Ma leaned close to me. "Ready?" she whispered.

I nodded and tried to look somber, but I was grinning inside. Together, we walked down the aisle to the back of the church. At the steps Ma greeted the minister, greeted everyone cordially, nodded, and spoke to each person. Yes, she agreed, it was a dreadful hot day, yes, wasn't it awful the price of dry goods, no, she hadn't heard from Jeffrey or Pa. Ma did all the greeting and smiling till every single last person had gone. When she was alone with the minister and me at the back of the church, she didn't waste any time.

"Reverend Hunting," she said, "who's going to minister to those boys out there in the fields? You know as well as I do that a battle is looming."

"Why, Mrs. Gordon, I pray for them unceasingly," he said.

"That's good," Ma said. "Now, who's going out in the field with them?"

"My prayers will be there with them," he said. "You can be sure of that."

Ma drummed her fingers on the reception table. "Reverend Hunting, that's not what I mean," she said. "My husband is out there. My boy is out there. Many boys are out there. If death comes to them, they need a minister of religion to see them to the other side."

"Oh, Mrs. Gordon," Reverend Hunting said. "Your son will come through just fine. I pray for him and your husband continually."

Ma pursed up her lips. "I pray too, Reverend Hunting, and just as like as not, what I pray for, the Lord doesn't see fit to give me."

"In his own time," Reverend Hunting said. "All in . . . "

Ma cut him off. "Are you planning to be in the field with them or not?" She pulled herself up tall, moved closer to him, staring him right in the face.

Like I've said, Ma's real big. Reverend Hunting isn't. He's skinny and narrow in the shoulders, kind of like a girl. Sweat broke out on his upper lip.

"If not," Ma said, "I'll go myself. I may not pray as good as you do, but I can hold their hands when they die. But I'll need your horse."

At that, Reverend Hunting pulled back, looking at Ma with alarm.

"We've given all of ours to the army," Ma said, which wasn't exactly true—in fact, wasn't true at all.

But, as Ma said, a little lie didn't bother her much at all.

"I'll make the supreme sacrifice," Reverend Hunting said, wiping the sweat from his face. "You may have one cow."

"Thank you, Reverend," Ma said. "We'll appreciate the cow. But we also need a horse. I know you have five."

"Four, Mrs. Gordon!" he said. Then he swallowed hard. He doesn't have a beard—Ma says because he's so stingy, even hair won't grow on him, and I could see his Adam's apple bob up and down.

"You may have the horse," he said. "One horse."

"And the cow," Ma said.

He breathed deep and then nodded.

"We'll be by tomorrow to get them," Ma said. She turned to go and then turned back to him. "By the way, it's not the 'supreme sacrifice.' Our men out there are doing that."

She turned, took me by the arm, and we left. As we did, she leaned in close. "Pompous hog!" she said. Together, we went down the steps, and both of us were grinning.

Chapter Eight

The horse Reverend Hunter gave us was a weary old nag, its ribs showing through its sides, its head drooping like it was ready to fall down dead at any moment. It would never do for Cameron. I asked Ma if I could choose another of the horses she had gathered, and she told me to take my pick. I chose a nice gray mare, and since we'd been given a few old saddles I took one of them, too, the best I could find.

I didn't get to do that right away, though, not for another whole week. Cotton was coming in, the fields covered with white blooms, and with slaves running away, we were real shorthanded. I did a lot of helping in the field that week.

I'd fallen into bed exhausted one Saturday night when something woke me, a scratching sound at my windowpane. Our house is low and long, and my room is right off the cobbled drive. I sat up in bed, squinting. Was that a face peeping in the window?

"Master Marshall, sir! Master Marshall, wake up."

Wake up? What . . .? I slid out of bed and padded to the window.

"Master Marshall, I needs to talk to you."

It was Matthew, Pa's groom!

"What is it?" I said. "What's wrong? Is Pa hurt?"

"Your pa's fine. I got a message for you. Come round by the porch please, sir."

"I'm coming!" I whispered. I pulled on some pants and tiptoed down the hall. Silently, I opened the door and stepped out to the side porch.

Matthew was standing in the shadows, holding his cap in his hands, turning it around and around like he was too nervous to stay still.

"Master Marshall, sir," he said. "I got a message for you, but it's not from your pa."

"It's not?" I said.

"It's from me," Matthew said. "They might hang me from a tree, but I'm telling you anyways. They done found out about your friend, about Hugo."

"Who? Found out what?" I said.

"The Rebels found out he's spying for the Union, and they's gonna catch him this very night."

"Catch him?"

"Catch him. Kill him most prob'ly."

"Matthew," I said. "I don't understand."

Matthew drew in a big breath and pulled himself up. He's a huge man, hands and feet as big as shovels, his neck as round and thick as a fence post. "Hugo is running around the woods with messages, spying for the Union. They found out. Tonight they's going to find him up on that hill, take his message, and kill him sure, slit his throat."

"What hill? And how do you know?" I asked.

Matthew just looked at me. "I know."

I just shook my head, trying to take it all in. Matthew was with Pa, on our side, the Confederate side. Hugo was spying for the Union. And the Confederates—us—we were going to kill Hugo?

"Where?" I asked.

Matthew told me then, told me about a tree on the hillside near Bull Run, a twisted, vine-covered oak. It was the place messages were exchanged.

"I'm telling you 'cause I don't know nobody else to tell," he said. "If you want to save him, you can. If you don't, that's your business. But if you do, you got to ride like glory. And if you tell anybody that I done told you, I'm a dead man."

"I won't tell," I said. "But what about . . . " I stopped, just looking at Matthew, thoughts running round like little mice inside my head. If I found Hugo, saved Hugo, then what about those messages? Did Hugo have messages that would harm us? Or help us?

It was just too confusing. But I knew this. I couldn't let them kill Hugo. I could *not* let them kill Hugo. I'd worry about messages after that.

"I should go now?" I said.

Matthew nodded. "Should'a gone a hour ago. But it's the best I could do."

"Can you saddle up Moscow for me while I dress?" I asked.

Matthew nodded and slipped off into the night, as silently as a shadow. It took me but a few minutes to get on clothes and boots, and I was ready. I had a canteen, and that's about all I needed. At the barns Matthew had Moscow all saddled up, and he handed me my reins. I leaped astride Moscow, and Matthew and I just looked at one another for a moment.

"I never saw you at all," I said.

Matthew nodded.

And I rode off into the night.

It was a ways to that hill overlooking Bull Run, the one we'd been at in the carriage that day, and I knew it wouldn't take long. But I was late, Matthew said, and I rode like the wind. I leaned into Moscow, and I didn't care that he was spooked of the woods. I rode him hard, and he seemed to know how important this was because he didn't once trip or stumble or try to brush me off under low-hanging branches like he usually does.

I never stopped, not even to rest Moscow, and I hoped he understood that I had to race onward.

Soon, though, the hilltop and tree came into view, and I slowed. God have mercy, I was frightened, my heart banging against my ribs. This was Union territory; Union men were down there below. But my friend Hugo was hiding under that tree.

I tethered Moscow under another tree close by, hoping he'd be hidden by the cover of night. I rested a moment, peering around me, and then went to the oak and ducked under the branches. It was dark under there, and it took me a minute to adjust my eyes. When I did, I thought my heart would jump right out of my throat—because under the tree lay a Union guard. Dead. And back against the tree, gasping for breath, his throat a huge open wound . . . was Hugo.

"Hugo!" I threw myself down on my knees in front of him. "Hugo!"

"Who?" he whispered.

"It's me, Marshall!"

"Marshall?"

"Yes, me, Marshall. Hugo, you're hurt. What happened?"

He didn't answer.

"Hugo! Can you stand up?"

Still, he didn't answer.

"Here," I said. "Let me help you. I can carry you." I slid my hands under his arms. "I'll lift you up. I'll put you on my horse. I'll take you to . . . I'll take you home, to Ma. She'll fix you up."

But even though I struggled, trying to heave him across my shoulders and up, he was a deadweight. With all the blood, he slipped out of my arms and landed heavily against the tree again. His eyes were closed, and his breath was making little gurgling sounds in his throat. He needed help. How could I help him? I'd just have to go for help, that's all.

I took my canteen and held it to his lips, but he didn't drink. I dribbled some drops onto his lips and then lay the canteen beside him. I looked around me. I didn't know what else to do. I had to go for help, and I had to find someone I could trust. The sun would be coming up soon. I ran for Moscow, untethered him, and leaped up. And as silently as a huge horse could ride, I rode away from that bloody place.

Chapter Nine

I awoke to the sound of guns coming from Bull Run, heavy cannonading from the river, mortars, and the roiling sound of heavy guns. I lay in bed, unspilled tears hot behind my eyelids, my head aching, and a pain in my gut. I had ridden away last night, ridden away from Hugo and that tree looking for help. I circled the Union camp below, looking for Confederates—any friendly Rebel soldier at all. There had to be one. I rode for at least half an hour before I realized something—if I found someone, if I found a Confederate soldier, he wouldn't want to save Hugo!

Suddenly, I realized what a fool I had been, what time I had wasted. Well, I'd just have to carry him myself, do it somehow and bring him back home. Ma would care for him, I knew. I rode back toward the hillside, and by then, the sun was coming up. And Hugo was gone. Someone had carried him off. Or had he been well enough to creep away by himself? I didn't know, but my head ached with worry and pain.

The day was hot and oppressive, and a feeling of dread seemed to lay on everyone. I didn't tell Ma what I had done—how could I say that I had been trying to help the enemy?—but of course, she knew something. I was dirty and tired, and most of all, Moscow was lathered up and weary. Ma didn't ask, but she surely looked me over hard.

We went to church, and even there, we could hear the sound of heavy guns, and after the service folks didn't linger, seeming anxious to get home. At home Ma paced and fretted, and it was so out of character for her that I was glad to get away. I'd bring Cameron his horse. That at least was something good I could do.

I tethered the mare behind Moscow and rode slowly to Claude's place. He was hoeing the garden when I rode up, and he looked up. "Hey!" he said, coming to stand beside me.

A whole flock of his little brothers came out, circling me and the horses, and Claude shooed them away. "Go, go, go," he said. "You want to get trampled?"

One little boy said, "Yes, sir!"

Claude just laughed and scooped him up and then deposited him back a little ways. "What do you have there?" he said to me.

"Something for your brother," I answered. "For Cameron."

"This here horse?" Claude asked.

I nodded.

Claude hollered into the house. "Cameron, come

on out here."

Cameron appeared in the doorway, a child tucked under one arm, a piece of hardtack in the other hand. "Here's your horse to go to war!" Claude said.

Cameron seemed so startled that, for a minute, I was afraid he'd drop the child he was holding. "For me?" he said.

He came flying down the steps, handing the little one into Claude's arms so fast that the child almost fell between the two horses. He leaped up onto the mare's back, untethered her from Moscow, and then kicked his heels into her side and flew off down the path into the woods. We could hear him hollering and whooping—and then silence. In just a few moments we heard him come tearing back.

"There's a whole mess of Confederate regiments down valley," he said, breathless. "I been spying on 'em every day for the past week. I'm going to join up with 'em."

"You can't join up just like that," I said.

"Why not?"

I thought of Jeffrey and the others and all the preparations. I wasn't sure what the rules were, but there must have been rules. "I don't know," I said. "Let's ride back and ask Ma about it."

Cameron shrugged, waved to his brothers, and,

together, we rode off. Cameron kept patting his horse and talking to it like he was just the happiest boy on the face of the earth. I studied him as we rode. He couldn't have been much older than me, probably just a year or two. From behind, I could see that his ears stuck out, and he looked a little bit wild, an old straw hat stuck atop his head, his skinny knees jutting out through his pants. I could tell he wasn't much used to a horse, though he rode well enough. He seemed to stop too fast and start too fast, and the way he patted the horse's neck put me in mind of a five year old who'd just gotten his first pony.

When we rode into the drive, Ma was there astride her own horse, looking solemn. She greeted Cameron kindly but waved off his thanks about the horse. "Things are going badly for us, boys," she said. "They're fighting at Bull Run, and we're getting pushed back."

"We are?" I asked. "How do you know?"

"Soldiers have been streaming back all day, starting early this morning. Haven't seen them myself, but many folks have. Seems they're being pushed back, and there's nowhere else for them to go but through the woods hereabouts."

Pushed back? Us? Our side? Suddenly, we heard a commotion, the sound of galloping horses. All three of us looked at one another. Confederates? Or Union men?

"Stay here," Ma said, thrusting out her hand. She galloped to the end of the drive and out onto the flats.

"Whoa!" she shouted to the oncoming men. "Whoa!"

Six or eight men on horseback were flying toward us. They wore Confederate uniforms, and they were filthy, soiled, and sweaty, and one of them was stained all over with blood. They reined in their horses, and one, clearly an officer by his uniform, spoke breathlessly.

"Who are you with?" he shouted. "Are you Rebs or Yanks?"

"We're with you!" Ma replied. "Where are you going? What's happening?"

"We saw the elephant, and it's not going well!" he replied. "We need a flanking movement underway, or it's lost. We're looking for General Beauregard's command. Do you know where he might be quartered?"

Ma shook her head "no," and so did I.

"I know!" Cameron said.

We turned to him.

"You do?" I asked.

He nodded. "Follow me." He wheeled his horse around.

"Whoa a minute!" the officer said. "Whoa!" We all reined in our horses. "Who are you? How do we know this isn't a trick?"

Cameron looked at the officer. "You don't," he said. "But it ain't. And my name, sir, is Cameron Crawford!"

He thrust his arm into the air as though holding a pretend flag or leading a charge. Then he wheeled around on his horse and took off, and without another word, the rest of us followed. I had no idea where he was going, but at least he had an idea, and that was lots more than the rest of us had. I figured this is what he meant earlier when he said he'd been spying on a troop of Confederates for a week.

We rode hard for about a quarter of an hour, heading west, away from home, and apparently away from the fighting because the sounds of battle became fainter. It seemed that we were making a huge semicircle around the fighting. We rode another ten minutes or so and then came abreast of a hill. There below us, spread out in the valley, was a huge contingent of the Confederate army. We all reined in our horses.

"God bless you!" the commander said, his voice soft, full of awe. "You've saved us, saved many. And

God willing, saved the battle, too." He squinted up his eyes at Cameron. "You know your way through these woods as well as any Indian. You want to join up, we could use a good scout."

"Then I'm the one for you!" Cameron said. He grinned at me. "Tell the boys good-bye. Tell them I'll be back when we whup Billy Yank."

The whole pack of them, Cameron, too, went thundering down the hill and into camp while Ma and I stayed on the hillside, watching. Far off in the distance we could hear the rumble of guns and cannons, and on the horizon smoke rose and stained the air, so thick that the sun was hidden.

Suddenly, below us, all seemed to be madness, men gearing up to march but some going this way, some going that. A few began taking down tents, and some were stamping out fires. A tall bearded man emerged from a tent. A bugle sang out, and all activity in the camp came to a halt.

"That's General Beauregard," Ma said softly to me. "Yes, yes, that's who it is. I wonder where your pa is."

There was stillness down below then as orders were called out. We couldn't hear the words, but the men began falling into formation, lining up, and marching out, seeming to know now just exactly what they were supposed to be doing. The ones in front were carrying flags—that same Confederate flag that had caused so much trouble in the tavern that night. We couldn't pick out Pa from among the others, but I could see Cameron. The last I saw of him he was turning to us with a huge wave of his hand. And I think he was happy.

Chapter Ten

The next morning the news burst upon us from all sides—we had prevailed. The Confederates had defeated the Union army at Bull Run. The Union army was, in fact, completely routed. Ma praised Cameron's skill and knowledge to the sky. We heard that because General Beauregard had gotten the message, he'd been able to make a wide flanking movement with his fresh troops. They had encircled the Union army on three sides till the Federals had nowhere to go but back—all the way back to Washington.

"Ma?" I said at breakfast that morning. "You think Pa will be able to get a message through today?"

Ma grunted and frowned, but she didn't answer. She didn't say so, but I could tell she was worried to pieces about Pa and Jeffrey. We both were. Even the darkies seemed worried. Rumors said that the battle had taken a terrible toll, with thousands of men dead on both sides. *Thousands!* It was impossible to get any news about what regiment was where, though gossip was flying. Neighbors came by with bits of information about this one or that one, but nobody had any news of Jeffrey or his regiment or of what might have happened to Pa.

There were lines on Ma's face and circles around her eyes. She said that she was determined not to worry unduly, and by the time breakfast was over, she had decided it was time to undertake a major housecleaning.

"Don't fret too much, Ma," I told her when I got up from the table. "We'll hear something today."

"Who's fretting?" Ma said angrily, which of course meant she was fretting plenty. She paced around the house all morning, barking orders at everyone and then changing her mind and taking back her demands. She was so unreasonable that I thought every one of the servants would walk out at once. Of course, they couldn't, but I surely wouldn't have blamed them if they had. Finally, when I thought I'd rather be in an army prison camp than stuck in this house with Ma, I overheard a conversation between Margaret, one of the kitchen maids, and Geneva, the cook. They said that newspapers were publishing lists of the dead. Margaret had heard it from her man friend, George, and he had heard it from a sutler, who said he'd seen the first lists himself.

As soon as I heard that, I knew what to do. I'd get the paper and bring it back. That way we'd know, one way or the other. Before I left, though, I made

Margaret and Geneva promise not to tell Ma about the papers till I came back myself.

Margaret looked at me, wide-eyed. "Mister Marshall, sir?" she said. "You must think I'm hoot crazy if you think I'd tell your ma anything today. I'd as soon put my woolly head in a gator's mouth. No, sir, not me. I'll not say a word to her or to no one."

I thanked her and then told Ma I was going to Claude's. I did something else then that I shouldn't have done, but at this point, proper things didn't seem to matter much anymore. I saddled up another horse, tethered her to Moscow, and rode on to Claude's, trailing the other horse behind. I knew Claude would be as anxious to learn about his brothers as I was to learn about mine and my pa, and this way we could ride in together.

At Claude's it took only a minute of conversation, and then Claude ducked in the house for a moment, came out, and the two of us were on our way. It was a hard ride to Manassas for many reasons, but the worst was this: soldiers, lost ones, Confederates as well as Union men, walking away from battle. From the way they were wandering, at first I thought they had simply lost their regiment or their sense of direction. But as we encountered more of them, I began to realize something: some of them had lost their minds. They were wandering wide-eyed, their faces blank, their clothing stained with blood and mud. Sometimes they spoke, begging for water, and while we still had some in our canteens we shared it. Once we saw a soldier darting from tree to tree as if still hiding from battle.

We rode on for another hour until, eventually, we came to Bull Run. There we stopped on a hillside overlooking the fields. The Confederate army had encamped where the Union army had been just days before. They were setting up Sibley tents, wall tents, wedge tents, a field hospital, a canteen, all of this amid the terrible signs of battle. Trees and fields were trampled and broken, stone walls were crumbled, and dead horses lay all around. Rain was just beginning to split the skies, and I know I wasn't imagining it, but the entire ground was so soaked with blood that it turned red as the rain coursed through it. As we watched, sometimes a body—or a part of a body—seemed to emerge from the mud. But the absolute worst were the stacks of bodies that lay alongside the hospital tents, flies covering them so that it was impossible to tell what kind of uniform the soldier wore, Confederate or Union. All around the hillside and the riverbanks lay bodies, the stench rising up along with the flies. *God, don't let Jeffrey be one of them, don't let Pa be one of them.* Ambulances tried to maneuver on the hillside, but it seemed hopeless as they got mired in mud—and bodies.

We watched awhile more in silence, and then we turned and rode on, neither of us looking at the other, both of us, I'm sure, thinking about our kin. It took another ten minutes or so to reach Manassas, where men thronged everywhere, women, too, shawls pulled over their heads against the rain. There was a crowd around the depot, and Claude pointed to the newspaper building up ahead. Throngs of people were pushing and pulling at one another. The paper must have been coming right off the press that moment, and hands reached out. Folks grabbed a paper and turned pages, and sometimes a cry went up. Women clutched other women as men elbowed their way in.

Claude and I rode into the throng, moving our horses carefully. Darkies were grabbing the papers being thrust out of a window, running back to their master's carriages, waving them in the air.

I tried to be polite, but no one was waiting their turn. When I saw my chance, I grabbed a paper, almost pulling it out of the grasp of another hand—whose I couldn't even see. Then Claude and I turned our horses and got ourselves to the edge of the crowd.

"Look for my brothers," Claude said. "Look for Crawford."

I held out the paper to him so we could read together.

"Tell me," Claude said. And then I remembered—Claude can't read.

"I'm looking!" I said. I scanned the list. The ink was still wet, and my hands turned black, the print running and smudging together, the rain making it all the worse. My eyes raced over the print, but I have to say, I skipped the Cs and looked for "Gordon" first.

Garrison, Gaston, Gerry, Grafton—no Gordon! No Gordon! Thank you, God, no Jeffrey Gordon, no Robert Gordon. My pa, my brother—they were alive.

I drew in a deep breath. Claude nudged his horse closer.

"Hold on, hold on," I said. I scanned the list again.

Cantor, Carey, Caster, Cramer . . . Crawford.

Cameron Crawford. He was there. He was dead.

So was Cash Crawford.

So, too, was Clovis.

I couldn't look at Claude. For a minute, I pretended I was still searching. I even thought of lying, of saying no, nobody's on the list. But no, that would be too cruel. Please, God. Maybe it was a mistake, how could they tell with all those bodies lying in piles? Maybe they had the wrong names. Cameron had joined up with no papers, no anything. Only a horse. A horse that I had supplied for him.

I took another moment, head bent. My throat was so tight that I thought it would burst, and my chest hurt. Why had I ever decided to ride here with Claude? Somebody else could tell him.

But who? I swallowed hard and then put my finger on the line of names. I looked up at Claude. Tears swam in my eyes, and his face seemed to waver in front of me.

"Claude," I said. I held out the newspaper, my finger on the names. "It's here," I said. "They're here. Cameron. And Clovis. And Cash. They're all here."

Chapter Eleven

My heart hurt for Claude, and it hurt for me, and even though Pa and Jeffrey's names weren't there, we knew the list wasn't complete. For two whole days we waited for more news. I kept telling myself and Ma that no news was good news, but still I worried something fierce. Surely Pa or Jeffrey could have sent a message. The woods and roads were streaming with men returning from battle, going from place to place. So why hadn't they sent a message—if they were alive? Or could they have been captured? Each day we pored over newspapers brought to us by passing men or by neighbors and were relieved each time that their names weren't there. Then on Tuesday morning we read that Jeffrey's troop, the 17th Regiment, had been moved upriver—and that he had been promoted. He was alive!

That filled Ma and me with joy, and for that whole day we just basked in that. Still, it was hard to be happy, what with worry over Pa and sorrow for Claude. How could you have *three brothers dead?* On Wednesday I rode on over to Claude's, and the two of us went out hunting, walking quiet like for a long, long while. Claude kept on shaking his head. I didn't ask. I knew. He couldn't believe, just like I couldn't believe.

On the following day, when we still hadn't heard from Pa, I decided I would go to camp and see what I could find out. With Pa being a general, not just a plain old foot soldier, it should be easy. I didn't even ask Ma's permission. I just told her I was going, and truth to tell, she seemed relieved.

She packed some razors and food that Pa might like and food for me for the journey. We both knew that I might not be back for a few days, but I promised Ma that the minute I had news I'd send word, and by noon I was on my way.

The woods were washed clean now after the heavy rains, though there were lost men lurking around and broken bodies still lying beneath the trees, surrounded by flies. I rode on, stopping occasionally to let Moscow rest, and it was late in the day when I reached the Confederate encampment. There were sentries all around, but no one stopped me. It was surely plain that the Yanks had retreated and wouldn't be coming here again any time soon.

I made my way down the hill, stopping and asking about Pa. Some men barely looked at me—a kid!—but others answered, even though they had no information. Then one of them suggested that I check the Negro quarters, where the servants and grooms might know something. Of course! Matthew!

Colored men didn't mingle with the soldiers, so if I went to the Negro quarters, I'd find him. It took over an hour of going here and there, but eventually, in the corrals, I saw him, his huge back bent over an a ambulance, washing it down.

"Matthew!" I shouted. I leaped down from Moscow and ran to him. "Matthew! Pa?"

For a moment, Matthew beamed at the sight of me, but then he shook his head, his big face twisted in pain. "Captured," he said. "He's in the hospital."

"Hospital? Is he hurt bad?" I asked, and I felt my heart pounding with fear—yet at the same time I was relieved—he was alive!

"Don't know, Master Marshall, don't know. It was late in the day when we rode in here, into the middle of the worst fighting you ever seen. Some say they saw a Union officer drag him away from the fighting. Then we hear he's in their hospital."

"Their hospital, where?" I said.

"Mebbe all the way back to Washington. Most likely in the field hospital back there somewheres." Matthew pointed behind him, vaguely.

Another of the grooms came up and spoke quietly to Matthew. They both looked at me then, like they were deciding whether or not to tell me something. Suddenly, I remembered Hugo!

"Hugo?" I said.

Matthew closed his eyes.

"Matthew?" I said.

"Gone," he said. "He's gone."

"Gone, like . . . ?"

"Gone to God," he answered.

It was all I could do to not burst out into tears. Hugo? Dead? It couldn't be. It couldn't be. I knew how badly he'd been injured but . . .

Matthew came close, bending over me and putting a hand on my shoulder, almost like he was my pa. "You done your best," he said softly. "You done what you could do. You should be proud."

"But he's dead!" I whispered.

"He's dead," Matthew said. "Now go on and see to your pa. Take that road back there, see?" He pointed behind him. "Arthur here says there's a Union tent hospital back two, three miles. They might let you in, you being his child and all. But remember, they's Union. They ain't going to take kindly to you." He tightened his hand on my shoulder. "Now, go," he said. "Godspeed."

I tried to thank him, but no words came out. I just nodded, mounted Moscow, and rode off, Moscow's hooves keeping beat with the thoughts in my head: Pa is hurt, Hugo is gone, Pa is hurt, Hugo is dead.

The sun was dropping below the trees, night

coming down, and my heart felt like a stone inside my chest as I headed on north. I had failed Hugo. I had tried, and I had failed. How could he be dead? And Pa—how bad was he hurt?

It was a long ride, miles of twisted roads littered with signs of battle and the passage of carriages and guns. After awhile the road became even more deeply rutted, and I began to see signs of a town, an encampment of sorts, the Union camp. Union soldiers were everywhere, some mending harnesses, some cutting up wood for fires, some cooking, some doing nothing at all. The moon was just rising above the trees as I trotted down the road looking for the hospital tents. No one paid any attention to me at all, and I finally found the tents, three of them in a row laid out end to end, with something like a corridor between. I didn't know if there was a prisoner tent and a regular tent, but since there were no signs, I just chose the one closest, hitched Moscow, and went inside. There were rows and rows of cots, side by side, so close you could barely step between them. Men looked up at me as I walked by, some of them pulling on my pants' legs. "Water, water," one man begged.

Two women were bent over a cot, nursing a man who was moaning pitifully, calling out over and over, "Mama, Mama!" Another nurse bent over a man with a pair of pliers or tweezers, picking maggots out of his wound. She looked up as I walked by.

"Ma'am?" I asked. "General Gordon?"

She just shook her head.

I kept walking between beds, looking down at each torn, suffering face, praying that Pa wasn't injured like these men, fighting back tears. So many of them were missing arms and legs, and flies were everywhere, on their wounds, on their faces even. The stench was impossible, and it was all I could do not to cover my nose with my arms. It was at the end, the very, very end of the row of cots, right against the tent wall, that I found him—my pa. His eyes were closed, his neck and face bloodied, a filthy bandage wound around and around his neck! I dropped to my knees beside him, taking his hand. "Pa!" I whispered. "Oh, Pa!"

I had barely whispered his name, but he opened his eyes.

"Son!" he said. His eyes, always a deep, deep blue, looked grayish, faded in the dim light of the candles. He squeezed my hand and then closed his eyes again. "Son," he murmured.

For a long time then he slept while I sat beside him, holding his hand, looking down into his face. I don't think I'd ever seen him sleep, really, and he looked different to me. I found a piece of newspaper nearby and began fanning him, trying to keep away the flies and cool him some. His face was wet with sweat, and his breathing was hoarse and heavy. Every little while, though, he smiled in his sleep, and I thought that was a good sign because it meant he wasn't in pain. Suddenly, he opened his eyes, wide awake, and lifted his head slightly off the pallet. "You take care of your ma, you hear?" he whispered.

"I will," I said. "But you'll be all right, Pa, honest."

Pa gripped my hand tight. "You're a fine young man," he whispered. "You surely have grown up. I'm proud of you, son."

"Pa!" I said, and tears began streaming down my face. "You'll be all right. Does it hurt?"

Pa lay his head back down. "Like the devil, boy. Now listen, take care of that cousin of yours too, you hear? Take real good care of Melody."

"I will, Pa. But Pa, listen, you're going to be all right. I'll help you. I'm here, Pa."

"I know you are, son," Pa said. "I know, and I'm awful glad of that. I think I was waiting for you. Now I'm going to sleep for awhile."

He closed his eyes then. He breathed in and out, deep breaths in and out, and once more, he smiled. Then, while I watched, while I held his hand, he wasn't breathing at all. My pa. My pa was dead.

Chapter Twelve

Uncle James found me by Pa's side and stayed with me through the night, not talking much, just being with me when he wasn't being summoned to care for someone. At daybreak we buried Pa, buried him along with 20 other men who had died in the night, and we put a little cross on his grave.

I didn't cry. I knew I would sometime but not now. Uncle James did, though, and I had never before seen a grown man weep. Uncle James sent a messenger on to Ma to tell her and then told me about Melody—told about himself, about how he had tried to save my pa—told me about all sorts of things.

I wanted to accompany Melody back home, but that, too, Uncle James told me about. Melody had refused, insisting she wouldn't have me or anyone else. Uncle James said he and General Tyler had agreed to that. It would seem more innocent, they said, just a girl riding home through the woods. But about this, I knew they were wrong. There was too much evil in the woods for her to go alone. Uncle James and General Tyler hadn't seen what I had seen. They had seen battle. They hadn't seen what was left after the battle.

Pa knew, though. *Take care of your cousin, take real good care.* And I would, whether she wanted me or not.

By late day, I was on my way, following Melody through the woods toward her home, my heart so heavy that it seemed even Moscow felt it, the way he trotted head down as though he was sorrowful. I kept a good distance back, but every so often, Melody stopped and looked over her shoulder as though she heard someone there. I didn't want to frighten her, but I couldn't let her know it was me—not after what Uncle James had told me. I knew she was furious with me. I knew she distrusted me. And me—well, what did I think of her? I thought she was just plain wrong, that's what I thought. And my pa was dead, and hers wasn't.

We rode through the afternoon and were close to home—her home—when I looked up and saw them. It happened so suddenly, so impossibly quickly, that I almost didn't believe what I was seeing. A troop of hoodlums on ragged, filthy horses, perhaps runaway soldiers, had appeared out of nowhere and were blocking the road in front of her. From where I was, a quarter of a mile back or so, I could hear their harsh laughter, see the old swaybacked horses, and I immediately realized they would steal her horse—or worse! I saw one reach for her, and she swatted his hand away. Within an instant, they had encircled her, their voices loud and scattered sounding, almost like they were filled with drink.

I felt for my waistband, for the gun Pa had given me. Could I really shoot a man? I didn't stop long to wonder. I just leaned into Moscow, digging my heels into his side. "Go!" I urged him. He shot forward, full of spirit once again. Up ahead, one of the horsemen was struggling with Melody, holding her by the arm, trying to unseat her.

"Stop!" I shouted as I pounded up alongside Melody. "Halt there! Let her go!"

"Marshall!" Melody cried. "Tell them to let me pass!"

The man holding her yanked hard suddenly, almost unseating her. She fought fiercely, flailing and yelling.

I whipped out my pistol.

Just then, a throbbing pain shot through my head, and I tumbled sideways as I was struck from behind. I whirled around, holding tight to Moscow's reins, fighting to keep my seat. A thug had wielded a tree branch, and he swung again, but this time, I ducked. I whirled forward again, the gun still in my hand. Moscow reared up, whinnying wildly and snorting as I leveled my pistol. Please God, make Melody hold still. Please, I'm a lousy shot, can't even hit a squirrel. And then for a blessed moment, Melody stopped struggling. I took aim and shot.

I hit him, hit him. Blood spurted, and he fell backward. Bedlam broke loose, men shouting, all of the horses rearing and stamping and whinnying with fear, two of them breaking loose and cantering off sideways into the woods, their riders holding on for dear life.

"Go!" I shouted to Melody.

She did. And I did too. I dug my heels into Moscow's side, and together, we raced through the darkening woods at top speed. Neither of our horses stumbled, though it was almost black now under the trees. Several times I looked back, but no one was coming on—probably couldn't, those old ragged horses being too worn-out.

It took about ten more minutes of hard riding, and then we were up on the flats, out of the woods and around the bend, and heading straight on for home. We slowed our horses when we could see the house ahead of us in the twilight. Lights were burning inside, and tall poplars on either side of the drive threw their soft, purple shadows. We trotted up the drive and reined in our horses, both of us breathing hard, our horses panting heavily. From around back by the slave quarters came the soft, sweet sound of the darkies singing.

Never had I been so glad to see this house. Suddenly then, I understood something, understood in a way I never had before about this war, about what Pa had been saying all along: this was our land, these were our homes. These were the homes we were fighting for.

Neither of us dismounted, just sat there catching our breath, looking at one another.

"Did you kill him?" Melody asked.

"That man?" I answered. "I don't know."

"No! I mean Hugo!"

"Hugo!" I answered. "Me kill Hugo? I tried to save him. I rode like the wind, the wind. I tried to get there before them."

"*Them?* Who? Who killed him?"

I just looked at her for a moment. "A Confederate soldier, who else?" I said softly. "Just like a Union soldier killed my pa."

"Your pa? Uncle Robert? He's dead?"

I nodded, swallowing hard. "He passed last night."

"Jeffrey?" Melody whispered, her eyes filled with tears. "What about Jeffrey?"

"His name's not in the paper with the dead. That's all we know."

Neither of us moved to dismount or even to trot farther up the drive. We just sat there looking at one another. What was I feeling? What was I *supposed* to feel? Wasn't I supposed to hate? I didn't hate. But God, I was angry. I choked back tears, thoughts tumbling over each other in my head. Thousands—*thousands*—of men were dead. My pa was dead.

"You saved me," Melody said at last.

I shook my head. "Pa did," I answered. "Before he died he told me to look out for you."

I turned away then and looked up at the house. Through the trees I could see the porch where flowers hung in baskets, the swing moving gently in the breeze. I could hear the sounds of harnesses jingling, of darkies singing, crickets and night creatures humming, a breeze whispering in the poplars.

Melody spoke quietly. "Will you stay awhile?" she asked.

For a moment, I couldn't answer. I watched as the Union flag, the flag of the United States, moved softly in the breeze above the house. Would I stay? I was a stranger here. I was a Confederate. This was a Yankee household.

But my Confederate pa was reaching out from death. Reaching out to both of us.

I turned to her. "Am I still welcome here?" I asked.

She smiled at me then, and in the smile I saw a hint of the girl I once knew, the girl from before this war, the girl I knew so well. "Foolish question, *brother*," she answered. "How could you not be welcome?"

I nodded at her. A blackbird flew overhead then, cawing, laughing it seemed, maybe laughing at us, as we turned our horses and trotted up to that divided house, that house that was home to both of us. A Yank and a Rebel. Together.

The Brothers' War

MELODY'S STORY

KINGFISHER
a Houghton Mifflin Company imprint
222 Berkeley Street
Boston, Massachusetts 02116
www.houghtonmifflinbooks.com

First published in 2005
2 4 6 8 10 9 7 5 3 1

LIBRARY OF CONGRESS CATALOGING-IN-PUBLICATION DATA
has been applied for.

ISBN 0-7534-5795-4
ISBN 978-07534-5795-5

Printed in India
1TR/0105/THOM/SGCH/90NS

MY SIDE OF THE STORY

The Brothers' War

MELODY'S STORY

PATRICIA HERMES

KINGFISHER
BOSTON

Read Melody's story first, then flip over
and read Marshall's side of the story!

Chapter One

"I hate this," I said, flinging down my sewing hoop. "I will not do one more stitch! Ever." I made a face at Elizabeth, my best friend in the world. She sat beside me on the swing, her embroidery hoop in her lap and her fingers nimbly going in and out with her needle and thread.

"You always say that, Melody," she said.

"I do not!" I said. "But I'm saying it now, and I mean it. Look!" I held up my embroidery. "It's knotted up and covered with blood from sticking myself with the stupid needle."

"Don't say 'stupid'," Elizabeth said, making pretty little stitches with her pretty little hands. "Aunt Josie will scold you if she hears that."

Sometimes I wonder how I can be friends with Elizabeth. She's my age exactly and so perfect it's frightening. She's good, and she's well behaved and ladylike—not at all like me. I think she's admirable. Sometimes. Other times I just think she has no gumption at all.

"Well, it is stupid!" I said. "Maybe if Aunt Josie hears, she'll say I don't have to do it anymore. I'm a failure at sewing."

"You can't be a failure at sewing, Melody,"

Elizabeth said, smiling. "Anybody can sew."

"I don't think a *man* can sew!" I said. "I have hands like a man. Look!" I held out my hands. They're not really like a man's, but they are strong. Mama always said it was a good thing to have strong hands, that it was the reason I was so good on horseback.

"Why, I believe even a man could sew if he set his mind to it," she said.

"That is definitely not true," I said.

"It is true. It's just that you're always in a hurry." Elizabeth took the sampler from my hands. "Here," she said kindly. "Let me see if I can get the knots out."

I let her take it. I knew that I was being unpleasant, and I didn't mean to be. It was just that I was worried and, to be truthful, a little frightened, too. Last night, when my cousins Marshall and Jeffrey arrived for a visit, they were all excited about the firing on Fort Sumter. Now that the Union fort had surrendered to the Confederates, Papa said it looked like there would be war. The boys said they hoped so, that war would be a lark. Papa seemed shocked, though he didn't say anything right away. Later, though, after supper, he came into the library where I was playing dominoes with the boys. Papa's a surgeon, and he told the boys that terrible things would happen in a war where brother would kill

brother. My cousins looked subdued, and they said, "Yes, sir," to everything he said, but I could see that they didn't really believe Papa.

I looked out over the fields. It was only April but was already hot, the sun baking the hard, red earth. "Look at Marshall and Jeffrey," I said, pointing across the lawn to where they were racing around with our groom and houseboy, Hugo, their horses in full canter, shouting and waving sticks at one another—probably playing war, even after Papa's lecture last night.

"Remember when we rode like that?" I said.

"Yes," Elizabeth said. "You do sit a horse well, better than any boy."

"Used to," I said. "Yesterday when the boys got here I begged Aunt Josie to let me ride. Of course, you know what she said."

"She said no, and she fainted."

I grinned at her. "Well, almost. She fanned herself with her little dimpled hands and asked for smelling salts. Isn't fainting the most foolish thing that women do?"

"Some women can't help it," Elizabeth said.

I wasn't so sure about that. "Anyway," I said, "after she recovered she said I could ride sidesaddle with Papa! Imagine. I know she means well, but she thinks

all girls are the way she is. I believe she's never been on a horse in her life. It's hard to believe that she and Mama were related, much less twins!"

"Well, she understands that we're twelve now."

"Imagine that," I said.

"You know what I mean," she said.

"Yes, I know exactly what you mean. When you're twelve years old, boys get to ride wild, and girls get to ride sidesaddle. Mostly, though, we sit on porches and sew. Last night, when Aunt Josie said that soon I'll be glad I learned to sew so I can make bandages for soldiers, I thought I'd scream!"

Elizabeth just gave me one of her patient looks. "It's not proper for girls to do certain things when they get to a certain age," she said.

"You sound like Aunt Josie," I said.

You're not a little girl anymore; more is expected of you. Aunt Josie says that 100 times a day, and Belinda, our housemaid, says it too. Belinda doesn't even want me playing with her son, Hugo, because I'm too grown-up now. That is just pure nonsense. Why can't you stay friends with someone you've been friends with since babyhood?

Elizabeth handed my embroidery back to me. "Here," she said. "I got all the knots out. Just go slowly."

"Thank you," I said, and I tried to sound meek,

though I was really still boiling inside.

Suddenly, there was a shout from across the field, and I jumped up. Jeffrey was circling around on his horse—circling around Marshall, who was lying on the ground! I leaped from the porch and ran toward them across the lawn. But I forgot that I was wearing fancy slippers, and I twisted an ankle, and down I went. I had just unscrambled my feet from my petticoats when Marshall jumped up, leaped on his horse, and all three began whooping with laughter.

"You didn't kill me!" Marshall yelled. "Just a wound."

"You foolish boys!" I yelled. "You scared me half to death."

They whirled their horses around to face me where I had stopped in the middle of the lawn. "Foolish boys!" I said again. "Scaring me like that."

"Come on, Melody!" Jeffrey said. "Get your horse and join us. We're looking for Yankees."

"Yeah!" Marshall said. "We'll hunt them down."

"These here boys think they can whup 'em," Hugo said, laughing.

Foolish boys playing foolish war games. But, oh, how I'd love to ride again! "I can't," I said.

Marshall trotted his horse over to me. "Aunt Josie won't know," he said.

"She'll find out."

"How?" Marshall said. "We had that big dinner, and she's resting. You know she always has a nap after dinner."

Yes. But if I got caught, Aunt Josie would tell Papa, and Papa would lecture me about how Aunt Josie is giving up a lot to come here and care for me, and I should try to be kind and listen to her. I do try, but I was aching to get on my horse again.

"Melody!" Jeffrey said. "Marshall needs you to teach him a lesson." He leaned down to me, speaking quietly as though telling me a secret. But he also spoke just loud enough for Marshall to hear. "You know how poorly he rides. Get your horse and show him a thing or two."

I smiled up at him. Jeffrey always teases Marshall. With Jeffrey being the oldest, I guess he feels he has to tease his little brother, but really, they're best friends. Actually, we're all best friends. I've spent so much time with them that they're practically like brothers to me—which is awfully nice when you don't have any real brothers or sisters. They even tell people that I'm their sister sometimes, just to confuse folks—something they love to do. And Hugo, even though he's a Negro groom, he's as dear to me as any brother. Hugo and I were born on the same day, and

we learned to walk on the same day, Mama used to say. We learned everything together—horses, hoop playing, even how to read. We learned other things together too, things that neither of our mamas will ever know about, like seeing who could spit the farthest.

Of my cousins, Marshall is my favorite. But Jeffrey is really handsome, and sometimes, lately, I even think I could like him as a beau when I get older if we weren't cousins. Jeffrey sits a horse much better than Marshall, too—much better.

But I was better than all three of them.

"Come on, I'll help you up," Jeffrey said. "We'll go to the barn and get Buster." He reached a hand down for me.

I looked back at the porch at Elizabeth. "Five minutes?" I called. "I'll be back in five minutes."

She waved, and if she was disapproving, I couldn't see it from here. I took Jeffrey's hand and leaped up on his horse behind him. He turned his horse, and Marshall and Hugo wheeled theirs around. We took off for the barns, my skirts waving wildly in the wind. I didn't care at all. Not about Aunt Josie. Not about modesty. Not about anything. I was up on a horse again. My arms were around Jeffrey's waist. For now, that's all that mattered.

Chapter Two

Hugo had kept my saddle clean and oiled, and he helped me saddle up. Then Jeffrey gave me a hand up, my skirts tied up like pantaloons. I turned to the boys. I had a thing or two to show them.

"Race you!" I shouted.

We took off down the rolling field to where the road began, then back around the house and behind the barn again, me in the lead. By the time we came around the front of the barn again, I was far out ahead. The sun was beating down on my uncovered arms and hands, and in my head I could hear Aunt Josie scolding me for sunburn—letting my skin get as dark as a common person. I didn't care one whit. I turned back to the boys, laughing.

Marshall and Jeffrey were bent over their horses' necks, and Hugo was standing in the stirrups, urging his horse on.

"Across the creek!" I shouted.

At the creek Buster didn't hesitate. I leaned into his neck, and we plunged over the stream, not even getting wet. I turned again, laughing. The boys were flying over the creek behind me. Where to next?

The woods. Marshall's horse, Moscow, hates the woods. Moscow deliberately runs under low-hanging

branches to knock Marshall off. He's done it dozens of times, and dozens of times Marshall has gone flying. But Buster knows the woods as well as I do, and he understands me, too. When we go under low-hanging branches, I let go of the reins and lie flat on my back, my feet loose in the stirrups. Buster would never take off running with me lying flat out like that.

Behind me, I could hear the boys whooping and laughing. Then, as we all moved deeper into the woods, the horses went more slowly, unsure of their footing. No racing here, but I did have a plan. It made me smile, thinking how I would hide and then ride out and spook them.

I guided Buster into my favorite hiding place, a dense stand of trees where low-hanging branches and vines trailed down so thickly that you'd never know anyone was there. It's a place I know from years of riding with Hugo before Mama died—before Aunt Josie decided I must grow up. Once inside the stand of trees, I stroked Buster's neck, whispering to him to shush, no snorting. His ears flicked back and forth, and he didn't snort, as if he knew we were playing a game, and he understood the rules.

After a bit I heard Marshall calling. "Melody?" I could hear them moving toward me.

I held my breath and stroked Buster's neck.

"Melody?" Jeffrey called. "You know we'll find you."

"There's a place somewheres about here she used to hide," Hugo said. "Or maybe it's farther on."

No, it's not farther on, it's right here, and you can't see me. I hardly breathed, just waited, trying hard not to laugh. I wanted them to be very close before I rode out, to show them how good I was at sneaking up on them. They came closer, and I could hear their low voices, though I couldn't hear the words.

I forced myself to hold still, whispering to Buster. After a few minutes I began to realize that they were moving away. I could hear branches and leaves crunching and hooves receding, then nothing—no horses moving, no snuffling. Just silence. I didn't have to wonder. I knew about these boys, and I knew what they were up to. On the other side of the stream, hidden by thick trees and undergrowth, was a path that wild animals had made for years by walking up and down the hill to drink at the stream. That's where the boys had gone, I felt certain. It was a place all of us had used for years. They meant to go up, then circle around and come charging down, trying to spook me and Buster out. But that path veers off a way into the hills. And the stream goes straight up.

"Okay, Buster," I whispered. "It's us against them, and we're smarter."

I dismounted and led Buster into the stream. I let him stop to drink, and then we walked in the streambed so that we made hardly any noise. At the top I led him out of the stream and into a grove of trees where I stood holding his reins, barely breathing. Soon I heard them, their horses plodding along slowly, coming toward me, so close I could hear their voices.

"Where'd she hide?" Marshall asked.

"Dunno," Hugo answered. They were so close now I could see them, their horses walking slowly through the brush, heading down the hill again.

"We'll spook her out," Marshall said. "Ready?"

"Hold on. Footing's bad here," Jeffrey answered.

I forced myself to wait, though I was about to explode with laughter. A minute later they filed past me, so close I could see the mosquitoes circling their horses' heads.

"Okay, Buster," I whispered. "Ready?"

He shook his head, but he didn't snort, like he'd remembered the rules. I mounted quietly, not making a sound. Through the thick leaves I could see Marshall and Jeffrey going on ahead, with Hugo bringing up the rear.

Slowly, softly, I led Buster up behind them and then broke into a gallop. "You'll never sneak up on the Yankees that way!" I shouted.

They whirled around, every one of them wide-eyed, frightened looking. Then all four of us burst out laughing.

"How'd you do that?" Marshall said.

"You should go into the army," Jeffrey said. "You'd make a great scout."

I made a face at him. "You all must be deaf," I said. "I was trailing you the whole way. Admit that I beat you."

"No. But I admit you were sneakier than us," Marshall said.

"Faster, too," I said.

Jeffrey laughed. "All right. Faster and sneakier, little sister, I admit it. Melody wins." He pulled out a handkerchief and handed it to me. "Best wipe your face before Aunt Josie sees you."

I took the handkerchief and wiped my face. The handkerchief came away filthy. Then I looked down at my feet—my very muddy feet in my very muddy new slippers.

"Oh," I said. "Aunt Josie will kill me. I'll have to sneak in the back way." I handed back his handkerchief.

"You sure you don't want to join Jeffrey's troop?"

Marshall said. "You just proved you're good."

"About time you admitted it," I said. "What troop are you talking about?"

"We don't have a name yet," Jeffrey answered. "Everyone's arguing over it and over what kind of uniforms we'll have. We don't even have an elected leader yet."

"It might even be Jeffrey," Marshall said proudly. "Pa's talking to his friends about it."

"Well, maybe, maybe not," Jeffrey said.

"Lucky," Hugo said. "I'd go if I could."

I turned to him. "Don't you ever say that!" I said it fiercely, much more fiercely than I had meant to.

He looked at me, surprised. "You mad at me or something?" he asked.

I shook my head. "No. But why do you think war is fun, all of you boys?"

"Nobody said it was 'fun,' Melody," Jeffrey said. "But it's not going to be bad. The Federals will see soon enough that we're not backing down. Look what we did at Fort Sumter. They turned and ran. This will be over before it even starts."

"You may not have said 'fun,' but you did say it would be a 'lark'!" I said, angrily. I turned away from them so I wouldn't lash out at them even more. My cousins were foolish, acting like it was a big, fun game,

and Hugo was extra, extra foolish. He, of all of them, should know how dangerous war would be, with some slaves already on the run and being hunted down in the woods.

But worse—and this is why I couldn't say more—if there was war, my cousins would be on the wrong side. Clearly, Jeffrey's troop was Confederate. Yet Papa and I—Mama, too, when she was alive—we all know one mustn't break up the Union. Papa had been really angry a few months back when Virginia seceded.

"I'm worried about getting back home," I said after a bit. "I've been away a long time. And I'm filthy."

"Go in the back way," Marshall said. "Me and Jeffrey and Hugo will take care of Buster for you."

We rode on back, slowly this time. When we got to the barn, Jeffrey gave me his hand and helped me dismount. It was hard to do with a skirt on, and he turned his head away like a gentleman. When I was down, I let go of his hand, and he turned back to me.

"Don't worry, Melody," he said. "It'll be all right."

I just shrugged. I knew what he meant. It wasn't about Aunt Josie finding out about me riding, either. He was talking about the coming war. But he was wrong.

It was not going to be all right.

Chapter Three

It was just a few weeks later that I awoke before it was light to the sounds of hooves pounding up the drive. Jeffrey and Marshall had gone back to their home in Manassas, so it couldn't be them out riding so early.

I got out of bed and went to the window, drawing back the curtains, wishing—hoping—that maybe it *was* Jeffrey coming back. Silly me, but I had found myself thinking too much about him lately, wishing he wasn't my cousin so he could be a beau. Now, in the faint light of the fading moon, I saw two men on horseback. They dismounted rapidly, and then, a moment later, I heard them on the porch and then in the front hall—though I didn't hear any knocking. There was the sound of excited whispering. One of the voices was Papa's. Who would come at this hour in the morning?

I opened my door and crept into the hall, peeking over the railing. I could see Papa ushering the men into the library, and then they were in the library, and Papa shut the door.

Oh, pish!

Well, I wasn't going to be left out of this! I returned to my room, slipped out of my nightdress and into a shift and a cool, loose dress, the first things

I could put my hands on. I didn't bother fixing my hair, just pulled it back and tied it with a bit of ribbon. Then, barefoot, I crept downstairs.

Now what? If I put my ear against the library door and someone caught me, I'd just die of embarrassment. But who was going to catch me at this hour? Even Belinda wasn't in the kitchen yet. And if someone burst out of the library, I could just say I was on my way to the kitchen looking for . . . what?

Well, who cared?

I crept to the library door and put my ear against it. There was murmuring, a hum of voices, and then I clearly heard the words, "They're coming closer."

To my astonishment, I recognized the voice—Uncle Robert, Marshall and Jeffrey's papa and my papa's brother! "We're going to need strong leadership," he said. "Thank the Lord that General Lee has come over to our side."

Papa murmured something that I couldn't hear.

"Yes, *our* side," Uncle Robert said. "James, I've been debating something for a long time. Please hear me out before you respond."

There was silence then, a long silence. Or was Uncle Robert whispering? Was he telling Papa something so softly I couldn't hear? I bent and squinted at the keyhole, but all I could see was the

desk in the center of the room. Good heavens, at least they could move into my line of sight!

Still silence—until Uncle Robert spoke. "In the morning I'm resigning my commission," he said.

"Good Lord!" Papa said. "You're not!"

What was happening? Papa never swears!

"I am," Uncle Robert said.

"I can't believe this!"

"Tell him why, Pa. Tell him what happened tonight."

Pa?

Was that Jeffrey? No—Marshall! What was happening? Something bad. I turned the knob and pushed open the door, and I didn't care how angry anyone got. At first, no one saw me. Papa and Uncle Robert were standing on either side of the fireplace, and Marshall was on the sofa, staring at the floor. Marshall was filthy—dark, reddish stains covered his shirt and boots.

"I can't hold that commission," Uncle Robert was saying. "West Point, our Union is dear to me, you know that. But Virginia is my heart, my *home*. It's *our* home, James, and . . ."

Marshall looked up and saw me. He made a little surprised sound, and then all three of them turned to me.

I looked from one to the other, my heart trembling inside me like a little bird. "Papa?" I said.

Papa reached out his hand, motioning to me to come to him. I crossed the room and stood at his side, and he put his arm around my shoulder, pulling me close.

"This isn't for Melody's ears," Uncle Robert said.

"It's all right, Robert," Papa said. "You can go on. With what you're telling me, even children will be part of this soon enough."

Uncle Robert didn't go on, though. He crossed the room and stood at the window looking out, his back to us. It was just beginning to be light outside, and birds were twittering in the bushes. A mockingbird began singing, so lustily, so joyfully, it seemed his heart would burst. For a long time we listened to the mockingbird outside and to the silence inside. Finally, Uncle Robert turned back to us.

"Something terrible happened tonight," he said, his voice low but seeming to tremble with anger. "The Union army took Alexandria, crossed the river, and set up camp right in the heart of our city! Marshall here, he saw the rest. God forgive me, I sent him down there."

"You couldn't have known, Pa," Marshall said, looking up from his hands. "You couldn't."

Known *what?* I could hardly stand the waiting.

"I won't make Marshall go through it again, so I'll tell you myself," Uncle Robert continued. "I sent him to the tavern to get information from my friend Jim Jackson, the proprietor. I think you know Jim. Well, I figured Marshall's just a boy, no one would suspect him of gathering information, and he's a smart boy, knows what to look for and what to report. He'll be useful to our side soon enough."

I felt Papa's arm tighten around my shoulder, but he didn't speak.

"Well," Uncle Robert went on, "some Union commander—Ellsworth, I think—was there. He went up the stairs after the Confederate flag—our flag of independence!—that Jim had flying up there. Ellsworth took down the flag." Uncle Robert took a long breath. "And Jim Jackson shot him dead."

It was almost proud the way Uncle Robert said that.

"How awful!" I burst out.

"Perhaps," Uncle Robert said. "And then Ellsworth's guard shot and killed Jackson. They both died at Marshall's feet."

I looked at Marshall, but his head was bent. I closed my eyes and leaned into Papa.

We were all quiet, and then Papa said, "I'm sorry for both men. But I can't understand your sentiments, Robert. How can you even consider fracturing this

blessed Union? I know your heart—we're brothers. You can't fight for all the wrong things!"

"I can fight for what's right," Uncle Robert said, angrily. "I'll use every ounce of my strength, and my sons will use their strength. We'll defeat this miserable attack on our homes, our flag, and our state. I'm sending my resignation in the morning. I'll do everything in my power to finance troops, to fight alongside my own sons, to give our own blood."

I looked up at Papa. Uncle Robert had gone to West Point and had a commission in the army. That's all Jeffrey talks about because he hopes to go to West Point too. So Uncle Robert was resigning to fight with the Confederacy? And his sons would fight with him!

"Robert," Papa said, and now his voice was not so much angry as sad. "It's sacred, this Union. Our grandfathers fought for this a hundred years ago! You know you mustn't destroy that. Listen to reason."

Uncle Robert stood a moment, looking back at Papa, but he didn't say anything else. After a moment he came to me, took both my hands, and gently pulled me away from Papa and into his arms. He held me close for just a moment. Then he released me, bent down, and kissed my forehead.

He turned to Papa then. He held out his hand, and after a bare moment's hesitation Papa took it. For a

second, they met each others' eyes. Papa's eyes were incredibly sad, and Uncle Robert—well, he just looked angry. Oh, please, I begged inside my head, please don't do this. They looked away from each other. Then Uncle Robert left the library.

Marshall stood up, and Papa went to him. He put his hands on Marshall's shoulders and spoke softly for a moment, so softly, I couldn't hear. Then Marshall turned away, went out in the hall after his pa, and left—without a word to me!

"Marshall!" I said. I ran out into the hall after him. "Marshall, don't . . . !" But he was gone. Gone.

Chapter Four

I came back into the library, my heart thudding hard inside me. I went to the long window and pushed it open, startling the birds into silence. After a moment they took up their chorus again, chirping and twittering and making their waking-up sounds, as if all was right with the world. Stupid birds. How could Marshall have been so rude, so—wrong! Was he really going to fight alongside his pa? Tonight he had been spying for the *Confederates!* And he hadn't spoken a single word to me! Yes, he'd seen two men shot dead. But still. And Uncle Robert—how could he do what he was doing?

Papa came up behind me and put his arms around me. I leaned back against him, and he stroked my hair. "You have such lovely hair," he murmured. "Just like your mama."

I nodded and swallowed hard. Whenever Papa says something about Mama, I still have to fight tears. It's only been six months since Mama died, and I think Papa still believes he could have saved her if he hadn't been off ministering to someone else that night—the night Mama got burned so badly with scalding water that she was fixing in the kitchen, getting ready to help one of the field hands who was having a baby.

"Papa?" I said. "Is Uncle Robert resigning to fight for the Confederacy?"

"Come, sit with me," Papa said. "Let's talk."

I shook my head and remained staring out of the window. "Papa? Jeffrey, too?"

"Yes," Papa said. "Jeffrey, too."

I turned around then. "Why? And even Marshall will be . . . be on their side!"

"I'm afraid so," he said. "Months ago President Lincoln declared a state of insurrection. But with what happened tonight, we may as well call it what it is. It's war, Melody."

"But why?" I said. "Why can't we stay one country? Remember what Mama always said?"

"Yes," Papa said, "Your mama would do everything possible to prevent the Union from fracturing. She was determined."

"Mama was determined about many things," I said, feeling that sadness deep inside me. "She would have said a thing or two to Uncle Robert and Marshall tonight!"

Papa smiled. "Remember when I took you and your mama to see the Capitol?"

I remembered. It was so beautiful, the flag flying high above it in the blue sky, Mama holding my hand as we looked on, all three of us almost breathless with the beauty of it all.

I took a deep breath. "It's just really foolish. If it's all about slavery, can't we just tell Belinda and Hugo and Roger and the field hands that they are freed people, just like Mama wanted? Everybody could do that. They could still work for us, couldn't they, if they wanted to?"

Papa went to the desk and picked up the framed picture of Mama. He let it rest on the palms of both hands, looking down at it. He does that often, as if he feels by doing that he can actually talk to Mama, that maybe she can hear his thoughts.

"I wish it was that easy," he said. "But even in the north some folks have slaves, and they don't want the slaves freed. They're afraid the slaves might take their jobs. Besides, it's not just about slavery. It's about different folks having different ideas about the rights of states. Some folks want slavery in the new territories, and some don't. But this I know: I revere this Union in my heart as well as in my mind. I'll stand by it. My brother is making a terrible mistake."

I turned back to the window. I saw a shadow then, someone running by along the ridge of trees. Hugo? It looked like Hugo.

"What's Hugo doing out there so early?" I said.

"Where?" Papa said.

"Right there!" I said, pointing. But when I looked where I had just seen him, he was gone.

Papa just shrugged. "Don't know. Probably doing some chores for his pa."

"So early? Running?"

"It's not important, I'm sure," Papa said. "The important thing is . . ."

I definitely saw Hugo dash by again, going the other way this time.

"Papa?" I said. "What's he doing out there?"

Papa just shook his head. "Doesn't matter, Melody," he said, waving his hand like he was brushing away a fly.

Well. I know Hugo, and I know Papa, and Hugo was up to something, and Papa knew what it was, and he didn't want me to know. I bet anything it had something to do with this insurrection or war or whatever they were calling it. But if Hugo could be part of it, I could too. Though Papa clearly didn't want me to know, I was surely going to find out. First, though, I had to ask this. "Papa?" I said. "Are you going to enlist?"

"I don't know. I worry. How can I leave you and Aunt Josie alone here with no man in the house?"

We didn't need a man in the house. Aunt Josie and Belinda and I could manage just fine. "We'd manage, Papa," I said. "We have Roger, and you know how good he is at running things. I'd be scared for you, though."

"I'd be safe," Papa said. "As a surgeon, I wouldn't be fighting." He grimaced. "Instead I'll be doing what I can to fix up all the ones they shoot apart."

That was a relief. But I had to ask the next thing, and then I had to go out and find that rascal Hugo.

"Papa?" I said. "They're *family*—Jeffrey and Marshall and Uncle Robert and Aunt Jem. You know how I love them all. Aunt Jem is my godmother! Can we still be friends?"

Papa looked down at Mama's picture again. "I hope so, dear one," he said, but it seemed more like he was talking to Mama than to me. "I do hope so. But it's only fair to tell you: right now I don't think that's much of a hope."

Chapter Five

Within a week everything had changed. Hugo was acting sly and important and wouldn't tell me what he was up to, acting like he didn't even know what I meant when I asked. He made me so mad that I determined that I would spy on him, maybe stay up all night one night and follow him. But before I could do that, even bigger things happened. Papa had left; he had enlisted with the Union army. President Lincoln had asked for a 90-day enlistment, and with the Virginia army stationed so close by, Papa said he'd be able to come home frequently—and soon. Elizabeth's papa also went off to war, on the Union side too, thank goodness. I don't know how Elizabeth and I could have borne it if one of our papas sided with the Confederates and the other with the Union. That was happening all over the county: women alone, the men gone off to war, and everybody taking sides, not just Papa and Uncle Robert but lots of folks.

Even at church, there were people who no longer spoke to other people who had been friends before, and that made Aunt Josie about crazy. She just could not understand this whole business about north and south and why we should fight at all. She was constantly getting herself into trouble, trying to be

nice to everyone, Confederates and Union people both. At church one Sunday she made the mistake of thinking Mrs. Adams was Union, when actually her two sons had gone off to fight with the Confederacy. Whatever it was Aunt Josie said, Mrs. Adams turned on her and spoke so sharply that poor Aunt Josie jerked backward, the ribbons on her bonnet shaking like trees in a hurricane. I had to take her arm and lead her outside, where I got her smelling salts and tried my best to soothe her.

Other things were in an uproar too. Roger acted bossy, not letting me leave the house, not even to visit Elizabeth. He said it was dangerous, with darkies running away, men chasing them, and troops of both sides everywhere. We rarely went to Centerville anymore, and so we had no way of finding out what was happening, not even a newspaper to read. A few times I debated sneaking off on Buster to see if I could find Papa or at least find a newspaper. I put that out of my mind quickly, though, because I knew Aunt Josie would faint into a heart attack if she found out. About our only outing anymore was church on Sunday, when Roger drove us in the carriage and I could visit with Elizabeth, but even there, children were excluded from the grown-ups' whisperings. On those days Elizabeth and Mrs.

Wilder came back with us for dinner, and Roger drove them home again later in the day.

I missed my long days with Elizabeth, missed the stories we made up, even missed our little arguments about being "ladies." I missed my times with Hugo, too. We once talked for hours, read books together. Now, though, he was busy at the barns with his pa, and when we did have moments together, he seemed different, quiet—worried even.

More than anything, though, I missed Marshall. His home is only a mile or two on the other side of Centerville, and he would often ride over for the afternoon. Now it had been weeks—and not a word from him. Was he out spying for the other side against Hugo—if that's what Hugo was doing?

At night when I was alone, I felt this terrible loneliness hanging over me. I lay in bed, the night rumbling with the sound of troop movements and cannons rolling just over the river. If the breeze blew a certain way, the smell of burning came wafting into the room. Other nights, everything was quiet, and sometimes that was even scarier. Was one side creeping up on the other? If so, who? Lots of people my age were in the army already, acting as bugle boys or messengers—even as spies! But that's because they were boys. Why couldn't a girl help? If only Mama

was here. On some of those nights I pretended to have talks with her, and I'd ask her what I could do. But of course, that didn't bring me any closer to an answer.

Then one day, after he had been gone for around three weeks, Papa came riding home. When I heard the hoofbeats, saw him galloping up the drive, I thought my heart would fly right out of my chest. I went running to meet him, and he lowered one arm and swept me right up. We cantered the rest of the way up the drive, both of us laughing, my skirts dangling most immodestly—and I didn't care one whit, and I'm sure Papa didn't either.

When we dismounted, Hugo came around from the back of the house, and when he saw Papa, he smiled so widely that I thought his face might split in half. Then Hugo took Papa's horse back to be rubbed down, and I stood back and looked at Papa. He was so handsome, so tall and slim and tanned dark from the sun. But so thin!

"Papa!" I said. "Don't they feed you?"

Papa laughed and put an arm around my waist. "Oh, they feed me enough," he said.

"Well, it doesn't look it!" I said.

It was a Sunday, so Elizabeth and Mrs. Wilder were visiting, and they came out to the porch along with Aunt Josie and Belinda when they heard Papa's

horse ride up.

"Well, I declare," Aunt Josie said, clasping her fat, little dimpled hands to her chest. She has dimples everywhere—in her cheeks, in her hands, probably in her knees, too, though I've never seen those. She hurried across the porch and raised her face to Papa when he came up the steps. He kissed her cheek and then turned to Mrs. Wilder, assuring her that he had seen her husband just that very morning and he was well. Aunt Josie began fussing, twittering like a little worried bird, about how if she had known he was coming, she'd have prepared a real welcome meal. Papa said it was enough just to be home—and to sleep in a bed for an hour or two.

"An *hour*, Papa?" I said.

Papa nodded. "Well, a few hours. Just long enough to rest and get some medicine. I have some in my chest upstairs, and they're desperately needed, things like salves, chloroform, bandages, morphine." I knew enough about medicine to know what morphine was for—pain.

"Papa," I said. I looked at Aunt Josie, at Elizabeth, at Mrs. Wilder. "Papa, are they really fighting in Manassas?" I knew I was speaking for each of us when I asked—because Manassas is awfully close to where my cousins live.

Papa looked from one to the other of us. "Well, Bull Run, near Manassas," he answered. "There's no real fighting at the moment, just skirmishes. But the Confederates are there, and our troops are nearby, and we're just waiting for orders to advance. There will be fighting, a real battle."

"When, Papa?"

"Soon," Papa replied. "Very soon, I'm afraid."

Aunt Josie put her hands to her chest, and Mrs. Wilder looked at her, eyebrows raised. I knew that look—Mrs. Wilder was asking silently if she should get the smelling salts. Aunt Josie shook her head, though her little hands fluttered around the collar of her dress. Her round, blue eyes were wide, fixed on Papa's face. "I absolutely refuse to faint," she whispered.

I didn't dare look at Elizabeth for fear we would both laugh. Yet somehow, it was endearing, too, Aunt Josie trying so hard to be brave. Papa leaned back against the porch rail. Suddenly, he seemed not so handsome anymore, tired, exhausted even. He was so thin, his eyes hollow, like a ghost had touched his face, and I wondered how I could have felt like laughing just a minute ago.

"Papa?" I said. "What about Jeffrey and Uncle Robert? Is . . . is his troop or regiment or—are they

at Bull Run?" I couldn't say, "Will he be shooting at you?"

"Don't ask that, Melody!" Aunt Josie said.

I looked at her, surprised. I had only asked what we all wanted to know—what I *thought* we all wanted to know.

"We'll talk later," Papa said. "Right now I'm going to go upstairs and wash up. And rest." He looked around. "It's just plain wonderful to see you all. You just can't know. When I come downstairs, I have some small presents for you all."

He started up the stairs, and Aunt Josie and Mrs. Wilder turned right away to the kitchen to work with Belinda to get supper prepared. I grabbed Elizabeth's hand and pulled her with me out onto the side porch where there was shade now that the sun had moved around the house.

"I'm so happy your papa is safe!" I said. "But why shouldn't I have asked about Jeffrey and Uncle Robert?"

"You know why," Elizabeth said. "Your Aunt Josie can't bear to think about it."

"Well, I can't bear to think about it either," I said. "But I have to. We have to. Elizabeth, do you really think they'll be shooting at each other?"

Before Elizabeth could answer, though, Aunt Josie

called for us both to help snap beans and do a hundred things for supper. Actually, I didn't mind because I wanted the same thing we all wanted—the very best meal we could possibly give to Papa. And maybe the truth was that I couldn't bear to think about them shooting at one another either.

Later, after Papa had rested and after we had eaten an enormous supper of ham and beans and potato salad and hot rolls and sliced tomatoes and corn pudding, we all retired to the porch to sit for awhile before Papa returned to camp. A few times at dinner I had tried to ask a question about the war, and once Mrs. Wilder asked a question, but each time, Papa answered by talking about the dreadful food in camp and comparing it to how wonderful our dinner was here. I really, really wanted to know about Papa and if he was going to be in the middle of real fighting and especially if he had had word from Uncle Robert. It was frustrating not to get answers or even to be able to ask the questions.

Now, out on the porch, he started handing out his gifts. Aunt Josie's was a sketch of a new five-car train from the Philadelphia, Wilmington, and Baltimore Railroad. It was an amazing train, huge and beautiful, and Papa said he had seen it, and it really did look just like it did in the picture. For Mrs. Wilder, there was a

song sheet with some new songs from the war: *The First Shot is Fired*, *The Girl I Left Behind*, and *Glory, Hallelujah*. And for us girls, there was a book called *The First Confederate Speller* and a booklet on arithmetic. Papa said it was perhaps strange to give us girls a Confederate book, but he had found it in a bookshop in Washington when he went to confer with President Lincoln, and he thought it would amuse us. It had been written by an association of Southern teachers and just published this year, 1861!

I turned the pages of the arithmetic book. "Listen!" I said, reading from it. "Seven Confederate soldiers captured twenty-one Yankees and divided them equally among them. How many Yankees did each Confederate have?"

"They had their hands full, that's what they had!" Aunt Josie said, and everyone laughed.

Soon it was time for Papa to leave, and this sad, dark feeling crept over me, the way you feel when a cloud covers the sun and everything gets cold for a moment. Aunt Josie handed Papa a package with biscuits and ham and a slab of bacon, and we all said our good-byes, trying real hard to be cheerful, though I'm sure all of our hearts were aching. I know mine was.

I walked alone with Papa down the steps to where

Roger and Hugo were waiting with Papa's horse, saddled and rubbed down and brushed.

"Will you come back soon?" I asked.

"When I can," Papa said, pulling me in close to him. "There are so many who need me right now and so few of us doctors. We don't even have a real hospital—we are housed in a church. There's so little of everything, Melody. I didn't want to say it back there on the porch because you know how sensitive Aunt Josie is. But it's awful. There aren't enough horses or food or medicine, and the real battle is still to come. Even when we know there's something out there, we can't get it. There are enemy lines to cross, things you'd never think of. We lost a skirmish and some men because a messenger was caught and killed, and we never got his message. It seems everything comes too late." Papa sighed and gave a little shudder. "I even had this nightmare when I slept upstairs before. I dreamed a . . . a young man back at camp was bleeding to death while I slept here. It was so vivid, so real, and I was too late to save him."

"But you save a lot of people, don't you, Papa?" I said. "And you have to sleep."

Papa smiled at me. "I do have to sleep, though at times I wish I could do without. But I'll come back as soon as I can, I promise."

"Papa?" I said. I had been wanting to ask this question, this more than any of the ones Papa hadn't answered before. "Jeffrey? His regiment? And Uncle Robert? Are they there to fight against you?"

Papa drew in a big breath and looked away. "It was Jeffrey that I dreamed about," he said quietly, staring off into the trees. "He was the one I couldn't save."

"Oh, Papa!" I said. "It was just a dream!" I reached out and took his hand. "It didn't really happen."

"I know," Papa said. "But the truth is that I don't know where their regiment is, though I presume they're close enough to be in the coming battle." He lifted my chin in his hand and kissed me. "I'll be home as soon as I can," he said. "Try not to worry."

He walked over to Hugo and Roger then. They were still standing under the oak tree holding his horse. The three of them spoke quietly. Were they talking secrets? I saw—I thought I saw—Papa hand a small package to Hugo. Money? Tobacco?

Or a *message?*

Roger and Hugo headed back to the stables. I watched them go, feeling rage rise up inside me. Why could Hugo do important things, while I could only stand and watch? Papa leaped up on his horse then, waved to me, and was gone.

I watched him ride away, watched till the drive

curved and I couldn't see him anymore, and then I turned and started back to the house. Already the drive and the fields felt empty and lonely without him. In my head his words ran around and around about how much was needed—horses, food, medicine. I thought about Buster then. For one awful minute, I thought about Buster. Should I let the army have my horse? That would be doing something important. Even the thought brought an ache to my throat, my chest.

For a moment, everything seemed a muddle, a big, miserable muddle, and I remembered something from when I was a little girl: I would flop down on the ground and beat my hands and feet against it when Hugo took a toy of mine and I couldn't get it back. That's what I felt like doing now.

Or then again, maybe I didn't want to do that at all. Maybe what I really wanted to do was smack Hugo upside his head.

Chapter Six

It was a few weeks later that I came down to the kitchen early. Belinda was there preparing breakfast and cooking up chicken and potatoes and eggs for a picnic. Mrs. Wilder had persuaded Aunt Josie to go out in the carriage to the hill overlooking Bull Run. There had been much talk at church about a coming battle there, and Mrs. Wilder wanted to see it for herself. I think she also hoped to see Mr. Wilder. At first Aunt Josie would hear none of that until Mrs. Wilder said she'd take her own wagon and go alone with one of her manservants. Then Aunt Josie agreed, probably because she was afraid to be left alone without any neighbors around.

Roger and Hugo didn't argue, but it was clear from the way Roger rolled his eyes that he didn't approve. I couldn't wait though. I was so happy to be spending a whole day with Elizabeth and to see where our papas and the armies were.

That morning Hugo was in the kitchen too, and it was obvious that he and his mama had been having an argument—obvious to me anyway because Belinda had that mulish look she gets when she's angry. They both shut their mouths when I came in, and Hugo turned away. Before he did, though, I saw his look, his

lip stuck out, eyes narrowed, looking so like his mama it almost made me laugh.

"Morning, Miss Melody," Belinda said. "What are you doing up and about so early? And with your hair not done yet?"

I put a hand to my hair. I had brushed it but hadn't twisted it up. Mama used to do that, and I had had a terrible time learning to do it myself. Aunt Josie always wants to twist it up for me, but I can't bear to let her. It reminds me too much of what I miss about Mama.

"I'll put it up soon," I said.

I looked from her to Hugo. "Hey, Hugo," I said. "What are you up to?" Like he'd tell me with his mama there.

"Mornin'," he said, without turning around.

"You just pay him no mind," Belinda said to me. To Hugo, she said, "You go on down to the barn. And the answer is 'no.' You stay there till we calls you for the carriage ride. I got no time to waste on foolishness."

"Yes, ma'am," he said. It was sullen the way he said it, but he went. At the door, though, he turned as though he was going to say something but then turned away again without speaking.

When he was gone, Belinda said, "Did you ever hear anything so foolish? A boy his age wanting a gun? What could he do but get himself killed?"

"He's got a gun!" I said.

"He's got himself a *hunting* gun," she said. "Now he wants a war kind of gun. One of them things you stick in your pocket and shoots off your foot with."

"Why does he want that kind of gun?" I said fiercely. "He's far too young!"

He was. But yesterday at church three boys in our Sunday school class were gone to the war—and one of them was only 11 years old.

Belinda nodded, a grim look on her round, shiny face. "Yes'm, far too young and far too stupid, a boy without no brain. Him sneaking back and forth in the night with that kinda gun? Why, if the Confederates catch him, they'll kill him quick as they'd kill a snake."

Aha! "What do you mean?" I asked, trying to sound matter-of-fact and not really interested. "Him sneaking back and forth where?"

Belinda got this sly look on her face. She turned away. "What you talking about?" she asked.

"You know! What you just said!"

She shrugged, still keeping her back to me. "Just talking," she said. "I talks too much. Now you go on outta here. It's too hot in this kitchen, and you is in my way."

She waved a hand and went on muttering under her breath, and it was clear that I wasn't going to get

any more information, so I went on out to the porch. I had been right! Hugo was doing something in the night—carrying messages maybe, like the one Papa gave him that night. I was right to pester him about it, and he was wrong to lie to me. Well, today he was going to tell me if I had to wrestle it out of him. I could still beat him up if I had to, though I would surely have to do it at the back of the barn or somewhere else out of sight of Aunt Josie. It almost made me smile, thinking about that.

Soon we had had our breakfast and were riding on out to the river. We went in two carriages, Roger driving Aunt Josie and Mrs. Wilder in Mrs. Wilder's carriage and Hugo driving the carriage with me and Elizabeth. We had made up a game called "Tall Tales," and we each tried to come up with a better story than the other. When it was Hugo's turn, he said he didn't know any stories because he'd never been to school—which was plain ridiculous. True, it's against the law to teach Negroes to read, but Mama was never one to worry about laws like that. She taught Hugo every single thing that she taught me, both of us together, and always, *always*, he caught on faster, except for one thing: he can't spell worth a hoot.

Eventually, he shrugged and laughed and told a story about a battlefield ghost. It was so real sounding,

with ghosts and soldiers sneaking through the woods, that he made me shudder, especially when the ghosts settled around a campfire smoking pipes made out of the ribs of dead soldiers.

In a little over an hour we came to a spot near Centerville where we parked our carriages on a hill overlooking Bull Run. Below us, spread out in the valley, was the Union army and not far away, just over the hill, Confederate forces. There were tents and men everywhere and, over on a wide field, a group of men practicing marching. There were fires where men were cooking, and some men were off in a field playing—could it be? Yes, they were playing leapfrog! There was no shooting or anything, just people milling about. I wondered if there really was to be a battle or if all the talk at church had been just that—talk—though both armies were surely there.

I looked around at all the many other carriages there. It was as if all of Washington had come out to witness what was going on—or maybe to spy and report back to their side. There were plain carriages and fancy ones pulled by matched sets of horses. Mrs. Wilder pointed out two carriages of gentlemen who were congressmen and one that belonged to John Nicolay, President Lincoln's secretary! Surely, he must have been there to report back to the president, and

that made me feel good.

And then I saw a carriage I recognized—Aunt Jem's carriage, Marshall and Jeffrey's mama! I stood up in my carriage to see better. Yes, it was her! And Marshall was with her! He was! I started to leap down, to go to them, but . . . but I hadn't seen Marshall since that night in the library. Also, though Aunt Jem has to be just about one of my favorite people in the whole world, would she even want to talk to me now? It just about made my heart ache, yes it did. But it didn't stop me.

As soon as Aunt Josie and Elizabeth and Mrs. Wilder got busy with spreading out food, I jumped down from the carriage and made my way among the other picnickers till I was beside Aunt Jem's carriage.

"Good morning, Aunt Jem," I said politely, trying to keep my voice from shaking.

"Melody!" Marshall said, and he jumped down from the wagon.

"Melody!" Aunt Jem said. "My dear, dear girl!" She jumped to her feet and leaped down from the carriage too, her skirts flying all around her. She pulled me close, almost crushing me in her arms. She held me away then, looking into my face. "How are you doing with all this madness going on?" she asked. "Completely insane, isn't it?" She laughed loudly and

hugged me again. "Oh, I've missed you these past weeks. But what can you expect with men running the world and deciding to go to war and messing things up?"

It was almost as if she was talking about some foul weather—or the colic in her beloved horses—the offhand way she spoke. She let go of me then and looked around. "Now where'd that son of mine go?" she said.

"I'm right here, Ma," Marshall said from beside her.

"Oh, that you are," she said. She turned back to me. "We're supposed to be spying, Marshall and me," she said softly, but there was laughter in her voice.

"Ma!" Marshall said, sounding shocked.

"Well now, it's no big secret—be sensible, look around you," Aunt Jem said. "Everybody in the county is out here, looking over everybody else. Good Lord, what's to spy on? They've built up an army, and we've built up an army, and they're all just going to line up and shoot one another dead. Now I don't say I don't have a favorite. I do. Robert and Jeffrey are on the right side. This is our state, our home, our slaves, our flag, and our property. But Lord a'mighty, what a dumb thing to do, go to war about it." She bent and pushed my hair back from my face,

looking at me closely. "Your papa doesn't think so, I know. What do you think?"

"Me?" I said.

"Yes, you!"

I was so taken aback that, for a minute, I could hardly speak. Aunt Jem always does this to me. She talks fast and loud, and she always says what she's thinking—straight out. It's what I like about her. It's what many people *don't* like about her.

"Well," I said, "I guess I think it's dumb, too, but . . ."

"Then we're in agreement on that!" she said. She put a hand on Marshall's shoulder and gave him a little push toward me. "You two go off and talk. I know you have things to say that you don't want me to hear, and I have people to talk to too."

She laughed loudly and turned away. She put two fingers to her mouth then and whistled, the way you'd call a horse in from the fields. Suddenly, a group of men on horseback came riding toward her as though they had just been waiting to be summoned. I simply stared.

Aunt Jem turned and gave me another look, grinning. "I know," she said, holding up her hand. "I know. I'm loud, and I have no class at all. It's what comes from being around horses all the time. Horses have no manners either, dropping their dung

everywhere and chewing and slobbering the way they do. But they have lots more sense than men do. More than women do too, for that matter."

I took a few steps away from the carriage and Marshall did too.

"Are you really out here spying?" I said, when I felt like I had caught my breath after Aunt Jem's onslaught.

Marshall shrugged. "Not exactly. Like Ma said, what's to spy on out here?"

"But you spy other times?" I asked because I was pretty sure that he did.

He just looked at me.

"You do, don't you?" I said. "You spy for the Confederates, right?"

"I might," he answered.

"You are so, so—*misguided!*" I wanted to use a stronger word, but even as angry as I was, I couldn't.

"I'm not misguided," Marshall said, his face flushed, angry looking. "You heard Ma. She believes in it, my pa believes in it, my brother believes in it. And I do too."

"You still think it's a big lark?" I said.

"That's not fair!" Marshall said. "No, I don't think it's a lark. Maybe I did a few weeks ago but not now. I just think it's something that we have to do."

"Your mama said it's stupid."

"She said it's stupid to *fight*," he said. "That's what she said."

"Well, you're fighting on the wrong side," I said.

We just stood glaring at one another. Suddenly, a part of me wanted to reach out to him, laugh even. This was so much like the fights we had when we were little kids and he took my toy or I took his, when we'd get furious and sometimes even kick one another. And then in the next minute we'd be laughing, be friends again. Now I started to put out my hand to touch his arm, but I pulled back. These weren't toys we were fighting over. He wasn't that little kid anymore. And I wasn't either.

I turned away, my heart heavy inside me, as I moved through the crowds and back to my carriage, where Hugo was unloading the picnic things. "Hugo!" I said, tilting my head toward the back of the carriage. "Come here, around the carriage."

Hugo swiveled his head around looking for Roger, but Roger had gone down the hill with buckets to get water for the horses.

When we were behind the carriage, I said, "Hugo, are you a spy for the Union?"

"What you talking about?" he said.

"You know what I'm talking about!" I said. "I've

been asking for days. This morning, after your mama sent you off, she told me that you'd been sneaking off in the night, and then I could tell she was sorry she said it, and she closed up like a clam."

Hugo grinned at me. "Hunting raccoon?" he said.

"Stop it!" I said. "Papa handed you something one night. I saw it."

He shrugged. "Money."

"I don't believe you," I said. "Hugo, Marshall is spying for the Rebels. He's right over there with his mama, with Aunt Jem!"

"I saw you with them," he said. "What'd he say?"

I shrugged. "Nothing. Except that he's on their side. I want to help our side!"

"Oh, no, Miss Melody!" Hugo said. "War's no place for womenfolk."

"It's no place for *men*folk either," I said sharply. "And since when is it 'Miss Melody'?"

He grinned again. "Since your Aunt Josie told me. You're all growed up now, she says."

"Yeah? Well, I can still beat you at arm wrestling," I said.

We were looking at each other eye to eye, and suddenly, we both burst out laughing. We've even grown at the same rate, though I've always been stronger than him. Also, though I hate to admit it, he's

smarter than me. "Hugo," I said, "if Mama was here, you know she'd tell me. She'd probably want me to help, too, you know that."

Hugo twisted one foot around in the dust and then looked up at me, his eyes sad. "I miss your mama," he whispered. "Miss her bad."

I nodded and swallowed. "Me, too."

After a minute Hugo made a motion with his hands. "I go here, there, through the woods," he said softly.

"Taking messages?"

He didn't answer.

"Could I do it?" I asked.

Hugo shook his head. "No'm," he said.

"If you can, I can!"

"Mellie," he said, using the pet name he had given me years ago. "Don't you see? It ain't the same."

"It is the same!" I said, feeling angry.

He shook his head and turned away from me then. Before he did, though, I saw the look on his face—sad, grown-up sad, and I felt this little tug inside my heart. "It ain't the same at all," he said. "Nobody suspects a little colored boy of knowing nothing."

It took me a minute to realize what he meant, but then I just sighed and closed my eyes. Yes. Yes, he was right, definitely right. Nobody would suspect a little

colored boy of knowing anything—just a little colored boy, raccoon hunting in the woods. It made my heart ache.

But then was it too much to hope that maybe no one would suspect a little *white girl* of knowing anything either?

Chapter Seven

I awoke in the dark that night and sat up, listening. What had awakened me? Guns? No. Yet something had awakened me. I pushed aside the mosquito netting that draped my bed, got up, and went to the window. I peered out, but even though the moon was almost full, it was too dark to see much of anything at all. All that was out there was blackness and the sound of crickets and cicadas calling and the river bubbling off in the distance.

The night felt hot and oppressive, and I pulled a wrap around me, deciding to go out on the porch where there might be a breeze. Quietly, I opened my door and went down the stairs, not wanting to awaken Aunt Josie. In the front hall the only light came from the moon that peered in over the transom. I opened the door, let myself out, and went and sat on the steps. The crickets and cicadas and frogs were busy, and the night birds too—mockingbirds, the only bird I know that sings at night.

I sat for awhile listening, enjoying the night sounds, the sense of the stars so high up above me, when suddenly someone slipped by me—a man, running softly around the side of the house toward the slave quarters.

My heart leaped to my throat. I pulled my wrap around me and eased back toward the house, scooting across the porch like a crab on hands and heels. Who? Was it a Confederate soldier? Or just a man on his way back from visiting his sweetheart? Or could it be Hugo? He had looked different from Hugo—not a Negro, I thought. But how could you tell in the dark?

I took a deep breath and then stood up and crossed to the porch steps. I stepped down silently and then made my way to the back of the house, running on tiptoes. At the corner of the house I stopped and peeked around.

Yes, yes, there he was, headed down the lane. I couldn't see too well from here, though it seemed he was heading for the end where the path turns toward Hugo's house.

Pish! I should have gotten dressed before coming down here. But so what? I could run like the wind. I'd sneak up on him, show him that he wasn't the only one who could go out and about in the night. He'd be more than surprised. I'd scare him half to death, maybe prove to him that I was capable of helping too. And if I was in my sleeping clothes, what of it?

I raced down the path, running quietly, trying to stay along the edge by the grass since I was barefoot.

I'd been down this lane often when Mama was alive, seeing to folks who were sick. At the end of the path I stopped. Nobody. I rubbed my foot where a stone had snagged me. Most of the houses were dark, folks sleeping, but in the last house, Hugo's house, there was a tiny flicker of light coming from the front window. Silently, I crept up onto the porch.

I knew it was rude of me. Folks were entitled to private time, not having people spying on them at night. Even Hugo was entitled to that. But—but I still stepped closer to the door—and stepped on something, something that yelped and jumped up, barking.

The light of a torch blinded me.

"Who's there?" Roger called. And then he said, "Miss Melody! What's wrong?"

"Nothing. Nothing," I said. "I'm so sorry. I—I saw someone running, and I . . ."

Belinda appeared behind Roger, her head wrapped in a rag, an old sweater pulled tight around her. "Miss Melody? Lord a'mercy!" she said. "Get in here, girl! You're in nightclothes. Are you—what you doing?"

She came and took my arm, almost physically hauling me into her tiny frame house. "Now sit here," she said, pulling out a chair for me. When I was seated, she hurried off to a corner of the room and came back with a shawl that she wrapped around my

shoulders. It was tender the way she did it, making little clucking sounds at me all the while as though she thought I was ill—and maybe I was ill, acting all crazy like this.

"I'm sorry, Belinda," I said. "Nothing's wrong. I couldn't sleep, and I saw Hugo, I mean I thought it was Hugo and . . . and I followed him here because I . . ." How could I say I was spying on him, wanted to scare him half to death?

Belinda reached out and patted me, and I noticed then that her face was creased with worry, her eyes huge and dark in her round face.

"What's happening?" I asked.

"Nothing," Roger said. "Nothing at all."

"Where's Hugo?" I said.

They looked at one another. Neither looked at me. Should I say it? Would I get Hugo in terrible trouble if I said what I knew, what I thought I knew?

"He's gone, isn't he? It's something about a message, isn't it?" I said, and though I was shaking inside, my voice was so calm it surprised me. "I know about it," I said.

They just stared.

"Hugo didn't tell me," I said, and that was the truth. "I asked him, but he wouldn't tell me anything. I just figured it out." I looked at Belinda. I didn't want

to say that partly it was because she was mad at him for going off in the night and wanting a gun. But I knew she knew.

"Something's happened?" I said.

"Nothing's happened to him, please the Lord," Belinda answered. "But he took off with a real urgent message, hours ago. Things got changed, and now we got to wait for him to come back and send a different message. Lord help us if we don't."

"But I just saw someone," I said. "Just now."

Belinda shook her head. "Hours ago," she said. "But he better get back quick before it gets light."

Well, I wasn't about to argue with them about seeing someone. I knew I had. But if they needed a message sent . . . "I'll go!" I said. "You know I can ride. If you'll tell me where to go, I'll do it."

Belinda pulled her mouth into a tight line and shook her head. "Go on off to bed," she said. "You ain't risking your life."

"There's no risk," I said.

Roger snorted.

"I'm just a child!" I said. "A girl. Who would think a girl could be a . . . a spy?" I wasn't even sure that was the right word. "A messenger?" I said.

"Never you mind," Roger said. "Seems like it's my job. If he don't come back soon, I'll go."

"No!" I said. "You can't. They'll think you're a runaway slave, and that'll be the end of you! I'm just a girl. Nobody will suspect me."

Roger ran his hands up and down his face like he was trying to rub off the tiredness. "That's just it," he said. "They would suspect you. What self-respecting girl would be tramping through the woods at night, less'n she was up to mischief? And believe me, once they decided you was trouble, they wouldn't hesitate to shoot you dead, girl or no girl."

I was quiet for a minute. And then I said, "What if I wasn't a girl? What if I was a boy?"

Roger laughed. But Belinda looked hard at me.

"I could wear Hugo's clothes. We're the same size," I said. "And you know how well I can handle a horse. I can catch up with Hugo. I could . . . "

Belinda had that mulish look coming over her, and she was shaking her head.

"Belinda!" I said. "You know how good I am on a horse. You know it. I'm way better than Hugo. Maybe I could even overtake him."

She kept on shaking her head. "Your papa would skin me alive if you got hurt."

"But I'm not going to get hurt. All I have to do is ride—wherever it is I'm supposed to ride." I held out my hands, smiling at her. "Look!"

Belinda's always telling me to put on gloves, that my hands are as calloused as a man's, and I should give up horseback riding. My hands were proof of how hard I can ride.

Roger leaned over and said something to Belinda quietly. She looked at him and then at me. Then she spoke to Roger. He nodded.

"All right," Belinda said, "but only because if this message don't get through, we's going to lose oh so many. If your Aunt Josie says yes, I'll say yes, too."

"Belinda!" I said. "I can't do that. She's asleep."

"Go wake her."

"You know that won't work!" I said because I knew Aunt Josie would almost certainly say no, and she might faint besides. "How about this?" I said. "How about I run down the road to the Wilders' and ask Mrs. Wilder?"

Belinda shook her head. "No'm. You ask your auntie. She say yes, I say yes."

"But you know her! She'll just say no. I can go and be back before she even wakes up." Belinda just shook her head again, that familiar mulish look on her face. She didn't even bother to answer.

I sighed. "All right," I said. "I'll go." I looked at Roger. "You saddle up my horse while I'm gone."

"You sure you can handle a horse at *night*?" Roger asked.

I grinned at him. I remembered Mama saying once that I was practically born on a horse. I knew that was too indelicate to say, though, so I just said, "I'm sure." I stood up. "I'll be back."

Outside, I raced back to the house and ran on tiptoes up the stairs. At Aunt Josie's door I stood for a moment, my heart thumping wildly. I realized that I was probably more scared of waking her and asking her than I was of the ride through the night.

"Mama?" I said, sending up a little prayer. "Tell Aunt Josie to let me do it." I quietly opened her door and tiptoed into the room, hoping to wake her carefully, gently. But before I had even crossed the room to her bed, she was sitting up, her curly, tousled head peering above the covers.

"Aunt Josie," I said. "It's me."

"What is it, girl?" she said. "What's wrong?"

I sat down on the side of her bed. As quickly as I could, I told her everything. I didn't make it sound all pretty, but I tried not to make it too scary either. I just told her that Roger said a message had to get through, that it was urgent, and that Hugo was carrying the wrong message.

She listened silently, and when I was finished, she smiled. "That rascal," she said.

"Who?" I said.

"Hugo, of course, and his papa and Belinda, too. I thought they were up to something. Carrying messages. Troop movements?"

"I don't know," I said. "They didn't tell me."

She sat quietly for a moment while I prayed as hard as I could—maybe not praying to the right person, not to God—but to Mama. *Let her say yes, please let her say yes, let me help. Let me do something to help—I know you'd let me if you were here.*

Finally, Aunt Josie looked at me. "I might be wrong," she said. "But yes, I think your mama would have said yes. Go on and Godspeed."

I was so relieved that I couldn't even answer. *Thank you, God. Thank you, Mama.*

"You be careful!" she said.

"I will."

She reached under her pillow. "Here," she said, and she pulled out a gun, a small derringer, and handed it to me.

I just stared at her. Aunt Josie with a gun—a gun under her pillow? Aunt Josie who faints over every little thing? She smiled at my surprise. "Sometimes you've got to stiffen your backbone," she said. "Learned that one from your mama. Now be careful with it. It's loaded. You ever used a gun?"

"Long time ago. At squirrels. In the woods with Hugo."

"Then you know what to do. Point it—and shoot. Doesn't take a bit of brains. And don't hesitate to use it."

I guess I was just staring at her because she laughed, and for just that moment, her light little laugh sounded just like my mama's.

"Be safe," she said. "Just use your head." She patted my hand. "Go with God," she murmured.

"Thank you," I said back. And then I whispered, "God bless you, too."

Chapter Eight

This is what I was supposed to do: I was to take the road to Manassas, the road I had taken so many times, the road that we had taken in the carriage to our picnic the other day. Once there, I should go to that double oak with the twisted vines and wait there. Roger said I couldn't miss the tree, and if I remembered rightly, it was the one where Mr. Nicolay had parked his carriage that day when we were picnicking. I was to tell the sentry that Hugo's message was wrong and tell him the code word—*snow*. That's all, just the one word—*snow*. Then I'd give him the note that Belinda had hidden inside my braid, twisted up on top of my head and covered with one of Hugo's caps. Though we realized Hugo might get there first, Roger said that wasn't important as long as they got my message. There was always another sentry there to give it to because that hill was guarded now—guarded by the Union soldiers.

Already I had a plan. I had gone through these woods many times, and I knew trails that veered off the main path, some of them shortcuts around small towns. On the way I'd watch for Hugo—not that any of us thought I'd really see him because if he heard a horse approaching, he was sure to hide. That made

me smile because with the way I was dressed, he wouldn't even recognize me. If there was enough light to see by, he might even think he was seeing a ghost of himself passing by. I was to ride as fast as possible, but I had sense enough to know that if I approached others in the woods, I'd ride slowly, ambling as though I was just on a jaunt, out hunting raccoons.

Those were my instructions, and I didn't ask Belinda and Roger how they knew what I was supposed to do or how they had found out that a new message had to be sent or even what the message said. They only told me that a battle was brewing—maybe even starting this very day. Belinda didn't say another word about it, but as Roger helped me up onto Buster, he said, "Ride swift now. This'll tell them where the other part of that Confederate army is holed up. If we know that, they can't sneak up on us, and we can beat 'em back."

That, of course, made me sad because who was on that other side? All of those other people that I loved. And was furious at. Like Marshall. Roger gave me a compass just in case I got lost, which, of course, I would not, and a water canteen. Belinda had made some sandwiches while I had run back to the house. Roger put them in my saddlebag and gave me an old

hunting rifle. It had a broken stock, but it looked good enough for a boy on a horse out hunting raccoons at night. Of course, I didn't tell them about the gun Aunt Josie had given me that was tucked into my pocket. Why worry them? Belinda would be sure that I would shoot my own self, and who was to say she was wrong? But it made me feel safer to have it. Less than 15 minutes after Aunt Josie had said yes, I was atop Buster and on my way.

It was dark in the woods, though the moon gleamed in places through the trees. The road to Manassas was completely deserted, though off in the distance I could hear troop movements or the movement of heavy artillery. The earth trembled under me at times as though a giant had awakened. Once in awhile the sky lit up briefly—perhaps torches lighting the way for troops. I had left home just after three, and I knew that even if I rode hard, it would take maybe two hours, longer by an hour than it had taken us before because of the dark. If that was so, I should arrive just around daybreak, even a bit earlier if I was lucky.

All around me were the sounds of the night—crickets, night birds, locusts, a seesawing rhythm as the creatures chirped, and, underneath it all, the hoarse cry of the swamp frogs. I peered ahead carefully, trying

to guide Buster on the safest trail so he wouldn't trip. At one point I switched from the dark path under the trees to the river path since there were fewer trees to block out the moonlight.

I figured I was just about there when I stopped to let Buster drink. I chose a spot near a thick stand of trees, took a sandwich out of the saddlebag, and ate half of it, just enough for energy. I was just finishing when I heard a horse coming toward me, its hooves thundering along the river path.

I looked around frantically for cover. I tugged on Buster's reins, pulling him quickly from the stream and into a nearby stand of trees. Was it Hugo? Or Confederate soldiers? Please, God, not Confederates. Roger said they'd kill me quick as anything if they thought I was a spy.

But I'm not. I'm just a boy, out raccoon hunting. Would they believe that? Did I look like a boy? Belinda had rubbed some dirt onto my face before I left and muddied up my shirt a bit. She'd smiled grimly when she'd done it, and when she was finished, she and Roger both nodded. "Ain't never seen a dirtier white child," Roger said. But was I dirty enough to be convincing?

I held my breath, waiting for the rider to pass by, staying as still as a statue. I stroked Buster's head, his

nose—no snorting, please, no, I whispered to him. And please, Lord, please, don't let it be a Confederate.

It was a Confederate.

It was Marshall.

He was bent over the neck of his horse, going at breakneck speed on the river path. I couldn't see his face, but I knew it was him, couldn't mistake his horse, Moscow, a giant, strong horse, racing along the open river path.

Marshall never saw me, never even slowed, just went at full gallop in the direction I was heading. Why? Was he out on a mission for the Confederates? But no, his home lay in that direction, just ahead. But why was he out in the night, racing like that? Was he the one I had seen before at home? Or had it been someone else?

I didn't have time to wonder. But I knew this: even if he was bringing news to the Rebels, he almost certainly wasn't going into Union territory. And I had a message, too, and I wasn't scared anymore. Marshall was a Confederate, yes, but he'd never hurt me.

I let Buster drink again, told him what a wonderful horse he was, and then I mounted him again, and we went onward. The night was giving up its dark, the moon receding. I wondered if I'd passed Hugo or if he'd taken a different path completely—and I

suddenly wondered if he'd passed Marshall. The road was widening now as it did when it got closer to the town, and I veered off onto the woods path again.

The sky had just begun to lighten, with a paler look over the horizon, when I came to the overlook where I was headed. There was no sign of anyone—no sentry, no Hugo. No Marshall. I reined in Buster, looking down on the scene below. There were masses of troops everywhere, hundreds of tents it looked like, though many men were sleeping right out in the open. Horses were cobbled together in a huge arena, and smoke from campfires rose into the air. I could see sentries posted around the perimeter, walking from post to post. I saw the field hospital, the church, where Papa was. I wished so much I could go to him, but I had promised not to—to only stop for the sentry at the rim of the hill, give my message, and then turn and ride straight on home.

I found the double oak tree and tethered Buster to a strong limb and then stood for a moment, feeling my heart thundering inside of me. An owl hooted from a tree nearby, and it made me jump. I felt a surprising surge of admiration for Hugo then. If he'd been doing this a whole lot, he was very, very brave.

I ducked under the vines, took off my cap, and wiped my forehead and neck, being sure not to

dislodge the note. It was dark under there, and I moved farther in, aiming to rest back against the tree. As I did, I stumbled over something, and I bent down.

It was all I could do not to scream. A man lay at my feet. The sentry! He wore a Union uniform, but he was sleeping. He was supposed to be watching, guarding.

"Sir?" I said.

No answer.

"Sir?" I said, a bit louder.

I bent closer and touched his shoulder lightly. "Sir, will you wake up?"

He didn't wake. What's more, his shoulder didn't even move; it was stiff and hard as if he was deeply asleep. Well, that wasn't very smart! What if the Rebels came through here? I knew only one way to wake him short of shouting, and I surely wasn't going to shout. So I poked him hard with the toe of my boot. "Wake up this minute!" I hissed at him.

He didn't. I bent closer, much closer. "Sir?"

He was dead. His mouth gaped open, and his eyes were open too, staring up at me. There was a huge hole in his chest, his uniform torn, blood caked all around it.

My head suddenly got a swimmy feeling, my eyes going all black around the edges, a huge black wave

moving in, crowding away the light, until I couldn't see. I backed away from him and put my head on my knees, willing the blackness to go away. I felt my heart thud up to my throat, my hands beginning to feel all tingly.

Don't faint, don't faint.

What to do? What to do? Dear God, what to do? *Use your head.* Yes, but what should I *do*? I had the message for the sentry—but the sentry was dead. And then, then I had a terrible thought: the sentry was dead. Where was Hugo?

Papa. I had to get the message to someone, and the only one was Papa. He'd know what to do. The sky was beginning to lighten quickly now, and soon the sun would be over the horizon. Hurry. Get down to the camp. But what if someone shot at me, another sentry?

Who had killed the sentry? Marshall? No, he'd never do that. Would he?

There was a sound then, a wheezing sound. It came from behind me. I whirled around. The wind moving the branches? Or maybe the soldier wasn't dead? It came again and sounded like breathing, heavy breathing. I squinted into the darkness, took a step, my heart thundering away inside me. And there, so close I could almost reach out and touch him, was Hugo.

He was sitting propped up against the tree trunk. Blood was caked on his cheeks, his throat, but his eyes were open, and he was looking at me.

"Mellie," he breathed. "Quick! To camp. Go quick."

Chapter Nine

"Hugo!" I cried.

I knelt in front of him and put a hand on his, and he squeezed it faintly. "What happened?" I whispered. "Did they . . . there's so much blood."

"Message. Tell them."

"Tell who? What?"

"Mellie, go," Hugo whispered. "Tell someone. The Rebs. They have the message."

"Hugo," I said. "I have a message too."

"Go!" he said. "Quick. Find . . . somebody."

"I can't leave you!" I said. "You're bleeding."

"Go!"

"I'll wait!" I said. "Another sentry will come by. Can't I wait for him?"

"No."

"Hugo!" I said. "Who . . .?" But I couldn't ask the question, couldn't ask about Marshall.

"Go!" he whispered.

I stood up and backed away a little.

"Wait!" Hugo said. "Don't." He struggled to get up, made it to all fours, but then fell back again.

"Hugo!" I bent to him.

"Don't go," he said. "They'll shoot you coming . . . to camp. You need . . . " He stopped, panting for

breath. "A uniform!" With his head, he nodded to the dead soldier.

I stared at him.

"Do it!" he said. "They'll shoot you."

"Do it? Put on his uniform?" I said.

He nodded and then collapsed back against the tree. Do it. Yes, I had to do it. I could see that. But I couldn't move.

"Hurry!" Hugo whispered.

I can do it—I can do anything—please God, help me do this! I took one more look at Hugo, but his eyes were closed. He was breathing, though; I could hear him. I straightened up and went over to the dead soldier. And I did it, the hardest thing I have ever done in my life. While Hugo slumped back against the tree, I took the soldier's clothes off of him. I lifted his dead body, my hands covered in blood, took off his undershirt, his coat, God, how could I, even his cap, and his curly hair fell all around, and I just closed my eyes to it, closed my nose to the smell of the blood, and when I was finished, dressed in his clothes, clothes that trailed to the ground, so big, so bloody, I stood up and turned to Hugo. His eyes were closed, and his breathing was raspy, burbling in his throat.

I realized there was one thing I could do for him, and I stumbled out from under the tree, tripping over

the pants. I got the canteen from my saddlebag, crept back, and then lifted it to his lips. He drank some. "Go," he whispered.

I left the canteen beside him and saw that one was already there. And I went. I gathered up the pants' legs and leaped up on Buster's back. Don't think, I told myself, don't think, the bloody clothes and the smell, don't think. And then I was downhill far enough, near the perimeter of the camp, and a sentry stepped out of the woods. I was ready to tell him who I was and what had happened. But he just waved me on.

The uniform, I realized.

The next sentry was at the base of the hill, and this one also nodded to me and then waved me on. The tent, Papa's tent. I could see it tall against the trees, a cross painted across it.

I rode straight up to the front, past men sprawled out on the ground, some still sleeping, some just rising. One rose up, saw me, and jumped to his feet. "Here!" he said. "Give me the reins."

The blood. Yes, he thought the blood on my front was mine. I leaped off and ran inside. Papa was sitting at a desk, writing in a huge book, and he stood when he heard the clatter at the doorway.

"Papa!" I said. "Papa!" And I ran into his arms.

Everything was muddled then for awhile. I know I

was sobbing, demanding that someone go and get Hugo, and Papa sent a surgeon and a stretcher up the hill for him. I told my story three times, four times, to three, four different men—General McDowell, General Tyler, others—and all the while Papa stood with both of his arms wrapped around me as though defending me from something. Maybe from myself because I could feel something scary mounting in me, horror, the smell of blood, and I could feel my voice getting higher and higher as I spoke. The generals pored over my note and the code word *snow*, and then, after I had told my story enough times, Papa told them that was enough. General McDowell shook my hand like I was a boy, a man, and he said I was braver than many a man.

Afterward Papa found some clothes for me, not a uniform, just plain clothes, way too big, but it didn't matter. Then he led me off, out of the hospital tent and across to another small tent in the shade of a tree, where he made me sit down on a cot. Then, very gently, very quietly, Papa washed my face and hands of the blood, talking softly to me the whole time, not about anything important really, just about things I had said as a baby, things Mama had done, soothing things, like about our summer garden.

I realized I was hungry, and it seemed so silly to be

hungry. I was, though, and yet by the time someone brought me something, I had fallen asleep on the cot. I actually fell asleep, but I don't know how I could with all that was happening, and I didn't even know how Hugo was. But I did. I slept.

When I awoke, the sun was high up in the sky and I could hear guns firing, heavy cannons, and outside, troops were milling all around. I jumped up and went outside. Where was Papa? Where was Hugo?

There was a sense of madness all around, of panic even. Men ran to-and-fro, carrying stretchers on which bleeding, broken men lay, stretchers that they set in rows along the front of the tent, and then they ran back again and up the hill. Other men hurried down, bringing more stretchers, more bloody men, and everywhere under the hot sun was chaos.

I pushed my way through the crowd, looking for Papa.

"Papa!" I shouted.

Through the crowd, I saw him. He was standing in front of the hospital tent, tending to someone, his shirt, his arms, and hands red with blood. As I came near, he called to me, "Help me here!"

I hurried to him, making my way through the crowds. He was bent over a table in the broiling sun, a kind of makeshift operating table, and on the table

was a man, his head and face a mass of blood, his beard caked with it, his throat an open wound.

"Hold this!" Papa said. He thrust a blood-soaked towel into my hands. "Hold it here." He pressed the towel and my hand against the man's throat. Then he bent and began work with scissors and a knife, cutting away at the wound.

The man's eyes were closed, and he moaned softly.

"Melody," Papa said quietly as he worked on the wound. "Melody, we're losing this battle. We're going to have to retreat. But your message saved lives, maybe thousands of lives. It told us where General Beauregard is bringing in replacements. We have to retreat to Washington."

"Where's Hugo?" I said.

Papa didn't answer.

"Papa?"

"I'm sorry, Melody. Hugo is dead."

"No, Papa!"

Papa's fingers kept going in and out of the man's wound, cleaning, sewing. "I'm sorry," Papa said. "I'm truly sorry. There was nothing we could do. He was dead before we got to him."

The man groaned and opened his eyes.

Uncle Robert! It was Uncle Robert!

"Papa!" I cried. "It's—it's Uncle Robert!"

"Chloroform!" Papa said, and he thrust a rag into my hand. "Yes, I know. Here, hold this by his nose."

I did, and I watched Uncle Robert's eyes close, his face get more peaceful looking.

"Hugo was brave, Melody," Papa said.

"But he's dead," I said. I truly thought my heart was breaking, the heavy feeling that shot through my chest. And then I thought of Marshall. He had been racing through the woods, probably with a message—to stop Hugo with his message? Did he kill Hugo? He wouldn't have. He couldn't have. Could he?

Papa bent over Uncle Robert, removed the chloroform rag, the blood-soaked towel, and then wiped the blood from his instruments onto a rag. He put a hand on his brother's shoulder for a moment and then moved on to the next stretcher where a young man lay—a boy, really. The boy was covered with blood and dirt, but he didn't cry out, just lay there, staring up at the sky. His leg was half torn from his body, the foot turned out at a cruel angle.

"Please?" he said, looking up at Papa. "You won't cut it off, will you?"

Papa looked down at the leg. He put a hand on the boy's shoulder. "I'll do my best, son," he said softly. He straightened up and turned to me then. "Melody," he said. "You can't get home today. It's too dangerous.

I'm going to send you on ahead with General McDowell. You'll be safe with him in Washington for a few days. I'll find someone to take you to him."

I looked around me. Men moaned and cried and begged for water. Flies covered their faces. Some men lay flat out on the ground in the broiling sun, not even on a stretcher. No one was tending to them. No one. And Uncle Robert was lying there soaked in his own blood.

"No, Papa," I said.

"You'll be safe," Papa said. "I wouldn't send you if I didn't think you'd be safe."

"Papa," I said, "I can't go."

"You'll be safe!" Papa said again.

"I know that," I said. "I just think—I'm already here. I should stay. You need help." I looked all around me, held out my hand. "They need help."

For just a moment, Papa looked at me while I looked back at him. "I can do it, Papa," I said. "You know I can. Please let me help?"

Papa drew in a deep breath. He nodded and then put out a hand and touched mine. "So like your mama," he whispered.

I bent over the boy on the stretcher then. He couldn't have been any older than me, 13 maybe. "What's your name?" I asked him.

"Sam," he whispered.

"Sam," I said. "My papa's going to fix your leg now. And if you let me, I'm going to hold your hand."

Chapter Ten

Things had only gotten worse, that day of the Battle of Bull Run. By five o'clock in the afternoon, the Union army was in full retreat, fleeing back to Washington. I heard later that Mr. Nicolay, President Lincoln's secretary, had been out watching the battle, and when he saw how bad it looked for the Union army, he rushed back to Washington to report to President Lincoln. President Lincoln ordered up more troops, but it was too late. The battle was lost. Two thousand Union troops were killed at Bull Run. *Two thousand!* Papa said probably that many Confederates had died too. Papa had managed to send a messenger back home, both to give the news about Hugo and Uncle Robert and to tell Aunt Josie I was safe and would be home in a day or two.

It was awful in camp when we retreated, made worse by the rain that began falling on Monday night. I worked with Papa through the night on Sunday and much of Monday and Tuesday. I hardly slept at all. I didn't cry, not once, and I did things I never thought I could do, holding men while Papa amputated arms, legs, stepping over stacks of limbs piled outside the tent. It was only when the funerals began, the slow drumrolls, the marching feet, men

marching with their bayonets turned backward, that I fell asleep. As I drifted off, I wondered how I could do it, how I could sleep. But these men were dead. There was nothing more we could do for them.

On the fourth morning Papa arranged for an escort to see me home. He actually suggested that Marshall might accompany me since Marshall had come to tend to his pa, who was now in the prisoner-of-war hospital. But I absolutely refused. My heart was just about broken, thinking of Hugo, thinking of how he'd been betrayed. Someone had killed him, someone who had wanted to get his message. And I had seen Marshall racing toward him ahead of me.

Anyway, it didn't much matter about the escort because after Papa conferred with General Tyler, they decided I'd be better off on my own. I'd be riding away from battle and going in the daytime. Even if there was a stray Confederate in the woods, I no longer had to pretend that I was anything but what I was—a girl on her horse on her way home.

It was late in the day before I started, and I rode through woods, all shiny now, the leaves washed clean, though all around me were the signs of battle. The trees and shrubs were crushed, clothing and shoes littered the forest floor, and I saw at least three or four dead bodies, flies and mosquitoes circling their heads,

the ants already at work. I didn't even stop to look at them. What had happened to me? Didn't I care? I felt as though I was in a dream, numbly looking on at things. Occasionally I thought I heard sounds behind me, footsteps or horse hooves, but when I turned to look, there was no one.

And then, I don't know where they came from. I don't know why I hadn't heard them. But suddenly there they were, a band of men on horseback thundering up to me. Within seconds, they had completely surrounded me, one reining in his horse right in front of me.

"What have we here?" the man said. His voice was rough and husky with an accent I couldn't identify, but it was surely deep Southern.

For a moment, I couldn't speak, my heart hammering away in my throat. There were eight or ten of them, all of them raggedy looking, some with rags wrapped around their heads instead of hats. Their horses were as skinny as skeletons, their ribs poking out, and the men themselves didn't look any too healthy. Their skin was dark as though they'd spent many hours in the sun, and their clothing was just tatters—rags and pieces of clothing and shreds of Confederate uniforms.

"Nice horse you got here," the leader said.

"You wouldn't have stolen him now, would you?"

At that, I got my voice back. "Remove yourself from my path, sir!" I said.

"Oooh!" he said. "Fancy talk." He looked around at his pack of men, a few of them chewing on grasses, all of them grinning. "This is a laydee we have here, gentlemen," he said, deliberately making the word "lady" strung out, fancy sounding. "A real Southern laydee."

"Don't think she's a real laydee, Charlie," one of the men said, addressing the leader. "No good Southern laydee is riding without a escort at this time of night."

Charlie turned back to me. "He's right. What is a laydee doing out in the woods at sundown with no gentleman by her side?"

"None of your business!" I said. "Now remove yourself!"

"Not until we get a good look at this horse, miss," he said. "Let's just check, see if this is one we been missing."

He put a hand on my hand—and I swatted him away.

He reared back in his saddle, throwing up his hands in pretend fear, but then he leaned closer. The other men moved their horses in too.

One of the men dismounted then and approached

Buster, put his hands all over him, rough like. Right away Buster did his little dancing step, shying away from those hands.

"Whoa, whoa, prickly, ain't he?" the man said.

"He's wild," I said.

That's when I heard another horseman approaching. The men did too, and we all spun around.

Marshall! Were these his men? His troop?

I turned back. If I spurred on Buster, could I outrun them all? Probably. Their horses looked about ready to drop down dead. Yes, but several of the men carried rifles, and one was armed with a club of some kind, a thick tree limb. But what about Marshall? Would he actually hurt me? I wasn't sure, but even if he wanted to, I'm a much better horse rider than he is.

He rode up and reined in Moscow right alongside me.

"If these are your troops," I told him angrily, pulling myself up tall in the saddle, "tell them to let me pass now!"

"My troops?" Marshall said. "They're nobody I know." He turned to the men. "What do you want with her? Now remove yourselves."

One man was looking over Marshall's horse, nodding and clucking. "Real nice horseflesh you got

here," he said. "I could take a real liking to this here one. A good horse and a gun, and I'm right back in business."

That's when I remembered the gun Aunt Josie had given me. I had done what she told me, carried it with me. It was in my waistband—but could I get it? Did I dare use it?

"Tell you what," Charlie said, turning to Marshall. "Why don't you two dismount now and let us get a real good look at these horses of yours."

"No, sir!" Marshall said. "We shall not!"

"Ooh, a little spirited, eh?" someone said.

Marshall moved Moscow up closer to Buster, so close their flanks were touching.

"It's all right, Melody," he said softly. "They're just hoodlums."

"Know what, Charlie?" said another of the men. "That laydee is wearing a right pretty ring there. Real gold, I bet."

Charlie smiled. His teeth were brown and broken, and I could see he had a wad of chewing tobacco in his cheek. He turned and spit—and not too carefully either. Some of the spit grazed my cheek.

Charlie laughed, and then he reached for me. He grabbed my wrist hard and pulled me violently forward, making Buster rear back.

Marshall whipped out a pistol. He pointed it straight at Charlie's head. "Don't. Touch. Her!" he said.

Charlie backed up, but he continued to hold tight to my wrist, twisting it painfully.

"Marshall!" I shouted. "Watch it, Marshall!" Another of the men was coming at him from behind, the one with the tree limb clutched in his hand. He swung it at Marshall's head, and Marshall ducked, and it whizzed past him.

Charlie let go of my wrist but, at the same moment, thrust himself forward and circled my neck with both of his hands, pulling me toward him. I fought back, and Buster reared up again as my arms flailed, trying to find the reins. I saw Marshall lift the pistol again.

Please, God, I prayed. *He's such a lousy shot. He can't even hit a squirrel. Please help.*

I held still a moment. Quit flailing. And Marshall shot.

Now flip over and read
Marshall's side of the story!